W9-DBK-956

Justice, My Brother

Center Point
Large Print

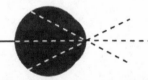

**This Large Print Book carries the
Seal of Approval of N.A.V.H.**

Justice, My Brother

A Novel of Oklahoma in the Early Nineteen Hundreds

Los Alamos County Library
2400 Central Avenue
Los Alamos, NM 87544

James Keene

CENTER POINT LARGE PRINT
THORNDIKE, MAINE

This Center Point Large Print edition is published
in the year 2017 by arrangement with
Golden West Literary Agency.

Copyright © 1957 by Will Cook. Copyright © 1958 by
Will Cook in the British Commonwealth.
Copyright © renewed 1985 by Theola G. Cook-Lewis.

All rights reserved.

The text of this Large Print edition is unabridged.
In other aspects, this book may vary
from the original edition.
Printed in the United States of America
on permanent paper.
Set in 16-point Times New Roman type.

ISBN: 978-1-68324-353-3 (hardcover)
ISBN: 978-1-68324-357-1 (paperback)

Library of Congress Cataloging-in-Publication Data

Names: Keene, James, author.
Title: Justice, my brother : a novel of Oklahoma in the early nineteen
hundreds / James Keene.
Description: Center Point Large Print edition. | Thorndike, Maine :
Center Point Large Print, 2017.
Identifiers: LCCN 2017002077| ISBN 9781683243533 (hardcover :
alk. paper) | ISBN 9781683243571 (pbk. : alk. paper)
Subjects: LCSH: Large type books. | GSAFD: Western stories.
Classification: LCC PS3553.O5547 J87 2017 | DDC 813/.54—dc23
LC record available at https://lccn.loc.gov/2017002077

For
Paul Rogers
who can hand, reef and steer

1

Because the day was Saturday, which was town day for us, I got up an hour earlier than anyone else and had the team hitched to the buggy before the new sun got around to showing itself. I'll introduce myself: Smoke O'Dare. Real name's Henry, but after Pa recorded it in the flyleaf of the Bible the family just forgot about it and called me Smoke on account of that's the color of my eyes.

Back there, on that day I was speaking of, I was pretty young, just past voting age, and not the kind of a young man folks took much notice of or even remembered once I'd moved on out of sight. To be honest about the whole thing, I ought to tell you right off that when people talk about the type of men they had in Oklahoma in 1903, they're not talking about me because on the tallest day of my life I never measured more than five-eight.

Never was called a runt though. Small-boned is a polite way to put it, but I'll tell you the truth: whatever flesh covered this frame had been pared down to solid muscle by two older brothers who believed that all the hard ranch jobs rightly belonged to the youngest.

And the O'Dare place was pretty big, or

considered so, now that Oklahoma had been opened up to the settlers for a year or so and a man's holdings were counted in half-sections instead of a dozen sections. Yet we O'Dares— Ma, Cord, Luther and me—claimed nine sections for our own, and I'm a little ashamed to admit that of all those sections only the first two were obtained in a manner completely honest. Cord and Luther were "sooners," sneaking in ahead of the gun to claim two, and within a year we bought an additional five from others who found the going too tough and wanted to move on with a little in their pockets to show for their trouble. Now before any of you start adding and figuring that I'm a paragon of honesty, let me tell you straight out that if Cord hadn't put his foot down and said that I was too young, there'd have been three sooners in the family instead of two. Of course, we'd been long-time ranchers in the Territory long before Teddy Roosevelt decided to open it, but that's not important now. Already I can hear you say that buying up a man's land before he'd proved up wasn't legal, and you'd be right. But the nearest United States Marshal was in Oklahoma City, nearly eighty miles away, and since he didn't get to our part of the country more than once or twice a year, there was really no one around who thought he ought to object.

Besides, there were others hogging all they could get too. Bill Hageman on the west side of the river spread out like thin pancake batter, gobbling up seven sections before we knew what he was up to. Still this left a lot of room for the little plowpushers who stuck out the dry summers and the danged grasshoppers, and the whistling winters. Fences went up, along with windmills, and schools and finally a railroad, which was the real reason Ponca City—that's our town—just didn't dry up and blow away.

Of course, at the time none of this concerned me much. Like I said, I was young and willing to get up early any time just so I could see the dawn's first light streak across the flats, or spend my evenings down by the river under the alders, watching the coral shades of the sky as the sun died. Cord, my older brother, said I was a dreamer, always whistling and keeping my mind so far-fetched he'd have to repeat a thing twice before I heard him. He may have been right; I wouldn't have argued it one way or another.

But to get back to what I was saying, by the time I had the team hitched and was heading for the house, Cord had come out of the kitchen door and was standing on the back porch, putting the final knot in his string tie. Cord was a big man, nearly six-one, with heavy shoulders and the kind of hips women admired so much, which was almost no hips at all. His hair was dark, as was all the O'Dares', a gift from an Irish father who had lived hard and died young. And Cord had the

O'Dare eyes, the shade of a prairie sky, a slate-gray with indistinct traces of blue.

When I stepped onto the porch, Cord said, "Put on your suit, Smoke. This is an important day."

"I was going to," I told him. I stood there beside him for a minute, watching daylight ripple across the flats, growing brighter every second. I guess I've always found a kind of magic in a prairie dawn and it always seemed to me that the light had so far to go that it couldn't come on you with a rush, like it did in the mountains, but sort of seeped in like a huge lamp slowly being turned up.

Cord's fingers fashioned a cigarette and while he twisted the ends, he said, "I guess you been wondering what's got into Luther, courting a woman by mail."

"I ain't been wondering a thing," I said. "If Luther wants a woman, then how he gets her is his business."

"You treat her decent," he said. Then, to take the bite out of the order, he smiled at me. His face was angular, almost roughly cast, but there was a handsomeness there that Luther and I lacked. It's hard to describe, but there was something about Cord that made men listen to him, even when they didn't particularly want to. And I guess a good share of women had given him considerable attention, because I'd heard it said—not to my face, you understand—that Cord was scared to fling a rock into the schoolyard for fear of hitting one of his own.

I guess there was a lot about Cord I didn't understand, and I knew I wasn't alone in my ignorance; some people had spent an unholy amount of time trying to figure him out. But that didn't make much difference to me. He was my older brother, and a handsome cuss who laughed a lot and treated me like I was man-sized, and when a fella is all of those things you can overlook a lot. His hair was as curly as kinked wire and a lock of it always hung down over his forehead. For as long as I could remember, Ma'd been brushing that lock of hair, and there have been times when other women have done the same thing, as though there was an irresistible challenge there that none could ignore.

"Luther up yet?" I asked.

"Up and fussing," Cord said. He laughed softly. "You go get dressed. Ma'll have breakfast ready in a minute. You don't want to miss the train, do you?"

"I guess I don't," I said and went into the house.

Ma was in the kitchen. I must have gone in the back door a thousand times and nine hundred of those times I'd found her in the kitchen where she spent so much time cooking for us that I sometimes felt guilty about eating, since I was the one with the voracious appetite. Ma was a heavy woman and didn't care if she ever lost a pound or not. Her face was like a melon, round and shiny-skinned, and her jowls quivered when she laughed, which was most of the time; I could never recall her crying about anything, except the day Pa died. His horse had gone lame and he was walking him home when he tripped and fell full-length on a rattlesnake. Cord found him and brought him in, and Ma had cried then, but not for long. She just gathered us together and said the O'Dares would have to shift for themselves from now on. And that's what we did. I was five at the time; Cord had yet to shave, but he somehow took Pa's place, and then some.

"We only got thirty minutes to eat and get," Ma said. "Get a shake on or we'll miss Luther's bride." Her eyes got round and shiny. "My, I'm so excited I don't know which way to turn."

I went into the hall leading to the room I shared with Luther, who is two years older, but who suddenly seemed a lot older now that he was going to get married. It seemed odd to me at the time how quickly family ties are severed by the prospect of matrimony. Luther seemed about to enter blissfully into what I considered to be a strange and somehow frightening institution. Until Cord gave Luther this girl's address, the four of us had gone along smooth enough, and I'd always managed to keep in step with the rest, whether it was rounding up half-wild steers, or riding after a bunch of pesky reservation Indians who had stolen two calves, or even standing back to back with Luther and Cord when we tangled with Bill Hageman's bunch. But now the whole thing was going down the chute and it made a man feel as though some kind of a door had been slammed in his face. Of course Luther kept insisting that nothing would change, but I knew different, having seen men get married. It always seemed ridiculous to me, how a man bold enough to tackle another man twice his size could get so meek and weak-kneed in front of his wife.

Looking back on this event a few years later, I could see that this was the first thing any of us had ever done on his own. The O'Dares had always stuck together but this was Luther's play, pure and simple, and we had to keep our noses out of it.

Luther was standing in front of the mirror, combing his hair for the fifth time although it was already as slick as a sweaty horse. He wore a white shirt with a ruffled front and his string tie had been carefully knotted. He looked at me, using the mirror so he wouldn't have to turn around. "We haven't got much time, Smoke."

"I've been told that by everybody," I said, peeling off my shirt. "You act like I was holdin' you up. Don't see why I have to fancy up. She's your girl."

Luther laughed, exposing white, even teeth. He wore a mustache, close-clipped, a dark line of hair that made his face seem broader than it actually was. His eyebrows were heavy thickets. "We got to keep up family appearances," he said. "Remember the O'Dare pride, Smoke."

"Sure, sure." I stripped off my faded jeans and stomped around in my long underwear, then finally got out my dark suit and pulled on the pants. "How do you know you're going to like her when you see her?"

"I'll like her," Luther said. "You saw her picture, Smoke."

"Aw, you can't tell nothing from a tintype."

He slipped into his coat and shrugged his shoulders. "I think you're more scared than I am, Smoke."

"Well, she's a stranger," I said. "How do you know she'll fit in?"

"That don't worry me none," Luther said gently. "You read her letters, Smoke. After that she couldn't be called a stranger, could she?"

"I guess not," I said so he'd feel better. But I still had my own opinion and wasn't about to change it. To me, Edna Shore was just a signature on a lot of letters, and a person can lie easy enough when you're a thousand miles too far away to call him on it.

I put on a white shirt, stuffed in the tail, then pulled up my suspenders. Luther went out and I followed, after picking up my coat and hat. Ma had the table set and a stack of wheatcakes on each plate. Steak filled a platter and there was enough coffee to float a small canoe. When we scraped back chairs, she went to her room, and by the time we were through eating, she came back, dressed for town.

I didn't have to look to see what she was wearing; I already knew. Cord looked past my shoulder and said, "That's right pretty, Ma." His smile was smooth and very pleased.

Then I turned around. Ma was wearing the velvet dress, the maroon one with the front cut too low and the waist pulled in too tight. The large-brimmed hat with the outlandish plume made her look like a music-hall prima donna. Around her fleshy neck were the beads, a color that clashed with the dress. Too many beads, and too bright and obviously cheap.

But these were all gifts from Cord and Ma wore them on every possible occasion, even going so far as to write in the Bible that she wanted to be buried in them, and if the undertaker would not let her wear the hat, to please let her have it in her hand like she was holding it.

I'll never forget the night Cord brought the presents home. Luther and I had to help him from his horse, and he slept the night in the barn, but in the morning he was sober enough to come to the house. Ma had been too excited about the presents to notice Cord's bloodshot eyes and for a week she had worn hat, dress and beads around the house. But finally Luther talked her into

15

putting them away, so she saved them for the weekly trips into Ponca City.

Now they were a landmark and Ma could be recognized miles away as she sat in the buggy, huge plume flying, beads reflecting the sunlight. For a time I wondered what kept folks from laughing outright; then once I saw Cord's glance sweep a gallery full of sniggering loafers and it became clear why no one laughed. Cord could look at a man in a certain way he had and make something that had been funny as hell seem not so funny at all.

"You was never prettier, Ma," Cord said again and got up. This was a signal for Luther and me, so I hastily finished the last of my wheatcakes. Cord left the kitchen for a moment and when he came back he was buckling on his cartridge belt and adjusting the double-action .44 Smith & Wesson on his hip.

"You think you'll need that today, Cord?" Ma asked. "After all, it's Luther's bride we're meeting."

Cord smiled and put his arm around her. "I'll keep my coat over it while we're at the depot."

He went out with Luther to get the saddle horses while Ma went through a last-minute fussing spell to make sure everything was all right. I held the door open for her and when she got ready to step into the buggy, I braced myself against the wheel so she could lean on me and hoist her bulk. The buggy listed heavily to one side under Ma's weight and I went around and got in. I sat there, holding the reins lax until Luther and Cord came from the barn. Then we drove from the yard, taking the Ponca City road.

The day was going to be another hot one, too hot for a coat and tie, but I knew better than to remove either. Cord and Luther rode to windward of the buggy in order to keep the dust off their clothes. Ma sat with her hands folded in her lap, the beads bouncing on her ample bosom, the plume nodding each time the buggy navigated a rut.

I've talked to a lot of people about Oklahoma and the plains country; a lot of them didn't like it. Monotonous, they said. Too flat. Maybe they're right, but I've always found a lot of pleasure in being able to look out and see nothing but miles stretching as far as I could see. Now I've been in the hills and in mountain country where you couldn't see from one ridge to the next, but I've never found a place I liked as well as the plains.

Ordinarily I'd be a little pleased and maybe impatient to get into town on Saturday, which was an easy day in this part of the country. A day when men got together over a beer in Lanahan's Saloon and talked about the weather and the price of cattle in Chicago, or what the reservation people were going to do about the Indians who constantly nibbled at the fringes of our herds.

And then there were the farmers, who wouldn't look at a cow unless they had a milk pail in their hand; the cattlemen left the farmers alone. That is, most of us did. Cord was pretty open with his dislike, but I sort of sided with Luther, who figured that every man had a right to his own way of life.

But like it or not, there was one thing we cattlemen had with the farmers; we were all as poor as rats in an empty barn. That may sound strange after my telling you how long we'd been in the Territory and how much land we had, but when the government opened this country to the homesteaders, we had to sell off everything and start all over. Sure, we lived in the old house, and ranched pretty much the same land, but it was a scratch start any way you want to look at it.

Getting back to that day, I couldn't find much pleasure in it. All I could think about was that by nightfall, we'd have one more in the family, or one less, depending on what kind of woman Edna Shore turned out to be. It kind of pecked me that Luther hadn't settled on a local female; there were plenty of them around. Some all Indian, some half, a lot of quarter bloods, and a few white that were single and fair-looking. But somehow none of them ever suited Cord as a possible sister-in-law. He never objected to Luther bringing one home, but only once. Cord would sit there and pick her to pieces. Subtle, you understand, but clear enough to discourage a girl from ever coming back. Cord was pretty good at putting his finger on a person's faults. He'd start in easy like, smiling a lot, and maybe making a joke or two, but in an hour he'd have that poor girl's weaknesses hung up for all to see. And by this time Luther would figure that he'd made another innocent mistake and take her home.

I guess that's why I was a little surprised when Luther took to writing Edna Shore, and more surprised that Cord approved of them getting married. In a way I guess you could say that Cord picked Edna, leastways he knew her from his Chicago visits. So with Cord's approval, Luther did his courting, not once clapping eyes on her except for that tintype he always carried in his shirt pocket.

Ponca City in 1903 was a sprawling, dusty place, and from a miraculous overnight blossoming, the town had finally settled down to some semblance of permanence. The first builders had flung up anything handy, but one winter of howling wind had leveled half the town, and the next buildings that went up were all solidly framed and heavily sided on firm foundations. The streets were wide for we're a breed of people who like a lot of room. All the stores flanking Cherokee Street had galleried overhangs to afford shade. I guess there was nothing about Ponca City to distinguish it from any other town in Oklahoma; you see one and you've seen them all.

But the traffic was brisk, being Saturday. Buggies were nosed in along the hitch rails, spaced by saddle horses standing three-footed, tails idly switching flies. And along the walk men moved about, or stood in close groups while the ladies presented their parasols to the drenching sunlight and went about their shopping. The children were all whooping it up at the school-yard, two blocks over on Elm Street.

I drove through the town to the railroad station sitting sunbleached and lonely by the cattle-loading pens and freight shed. The tracks stretched away as far as the eye could see, reflecting the sun's smashing light. Pulling in along the shady side, I dismounted and helped Ma down. She adjusted the velvet dress, patted her beads, then straightened the huge hat. Afterward she just stood there, her face patient and composed.

Cord consulted the watch that had been Father's. "Time for a glass of beer at Lanahan's. You stay with Ma, Smoke."

"It's my place to stay," Luther said quickly and dismounted. He handed the reins to me and I stepped into the saddle. When Cord turned toward the main drag, I sided him. We tied up before Lanahan's Saloon and Cord paused for his look up and down the street. He ducked under the hitch rail and I followed him across the walk to

Lanahan's broad porch. The louvered doors were slack and Cord took a look inside while his right hand brushed back the tail of his coat, exposing the double-action .44 in its swivel holster.

I'd always wondered what made Cord do that, for the day was nearly gone when a man carried a gun on his hip. And it was rarer still to see a holster all cut away or hung on a rivet. But this was one of Cord O'Dare's little quirks and after a while folks around our part of Oklahoma got used to seeing the gun and listening to Cord tell how he could knock the knot out of a pine board at twenty-five feet, or watching him demonstrate this at the biannual Ponca City Volunteer Fire Brigade beer party. Where Cord was concerned, you could count on one thing: he always did what he said he'd do, whether that was paying back money he'd borrowed or loosening a man's front teeth. All of which might have been added reason for folks not objecting to the way Cord packed his .44.

Pete Lanahan was finding business brisk; at least two dozen men cluttered the place. Most of them were farmers, and therefore virtual strangers. I nodded to them but Cord didn't even glance their way. He pressed on to the bar and I followed. Lige Bingham and Vince Randolf sat at one of the tables, talking to three other farmers. They looked at me and I spoke, figuring that it didn't cost anything to be civil.

"Beer here," Cord said and Pete Lanahan came down the length of the bar, his hands working the mugs and taps. He shaved the head off two beers with a wooden paddle, then slid them along the cherrywood.

"Train going to be on time, Cord?"

"Nothing to make it late," Cord said. He drank some of his beer, then wiped the foam mustache from his upper lip.

"That Luther's one for takin' a chance, ain't he?" Lanahan grinned. "I'd never marry a woman I never seen."

"It's his gamble," Cord said. "Suppose you let him take it, Pete." He lifted his beer then and turned, hooking his elbows on the edge of the bar. Lige Bingham and Vince Randolf were watching him.

Finally Cord asked, "A little dry out your way?"

We all knew danged good and well that it was; the farmers' tongues were hanging out for water, and since our spread and Bill Hageman's ran on both banks of the river for three miles, there wasn't much chance of their getting any. This isn't to say that either Hageman or the O'Dares owned all the land, but we'd been careful to get the sections that controlled the water. The truth of the matter was, we'd lived here long enough to know that water was more important than grass and only the farmers who'd dug a well and put up a windmill were even getting by.

If Cord had had his way about it, we'd have owned all the land along the river, and then some, but in order to control as much as we did, we had to give up some to the farmers; they owned sections and put up fences right in the middle of our grazing land, which was a constant irritation to Cord. And I guess Bill Hageman didn't like it much either, but neither of them had done anything about it.

Lige Bingham acted like he wasn't going to answer. Then he said, "I could use rain." He raised a hand and brushed his heavy mustache. He had no love for the O'Dares, or any cattleman for that matter. The talk was that he'd been moved twice at the point of a Winchester and he swore he'd never be moved again. Which was all right; I'd probably feel the same way if I were in his shoes, but a man gets a little tired of being glared at all the time just because he'd rather butcher a steer than milk a cow.

"If it gets too dry for you," Cord said mildly, "I'll buy you out."

"I'm not selling," Bingham said. "The land's good and if we could dig a few irrigation ditches, we'd make out."

"Dig a well," Cord suggested.

"That takes money," Bingham pointed out. "If we could irrigate for a year, we'd make enough to put down a well."

Cord sipped his beer slowly. I watched him for

I had seen him do this before, encourage a man to argue and plead his case when all the time he had made up his mind to turn him down. "What does Bill Hageman say about irrigating?"

"He ain't against it," Lige Bingham stated.

There wasn't much Cord could do about Bingham for the man had his land snuggled amongst Bill Hageman's spread. But Vince Randolf was another matter. He was one of the three farmers that cut up our property. Cord switched his attention to him and asked, "You thinking of irrigating too?"

"I was," Randolf admitted.

"You're not against the river," Cord reminded him. "Neither is Higgins, Mooney, or Everett. I'd hate to have ditches dug across my land. I'd hate to see the river lowered just so's you could grow a crop and have the frost kill it." He said this slow and careful so there would be no misunderstanding.

And Vince Randolf understood. He looked at Bingham, then said, "I don't like being surrounded by your property any more than you like me being there. It grates me to drive across another man's land to get to my own."

"I'll buy you out," Cord said. "A fair price."

"Thank you, no," Randolf said flatly.

Cord shrugged and finished his beer, then indicated that I ought to do the same. As he stepped toward the door, the train whistle sounded faintly, blowing for Rindo's Springs a far piece down the road.

We stood for a moment on Lanahan's front porch, watching a buggy and rider come in from the east. I glanced quickly at Cord, then whipped my attention back to the buggy, which Julie Hageman was driving. She was a year older than me, but I sure never counted that little difference as any great obstacle. She was a slender girl, almost as tall as I am, and I didn't object to that either. The fact is, there wasn't much about Julie Hageman that I did object to, even the way she would look right through me to see Cord. Her hair was auburn, or it was in the wintertime when there was little sun to bleach it an exciting shade of red. Her eyes were dark and throughout a year I averaged up a lot of wasted time just dreaming about how they would look when she confessed that it was me she loved.

The buggy wheeled by and Cord removed his hat, bowing slightly to Julie. It was then that I looked at her brother, Bill, on his big bay. From beneath his hat brim came a glance as heavy as thunder, then he passed on to dismount in front of Herschammer's Hardware. I stepped down, ready to go on to the depot, but Cord put his hand on my shoulder.

"Wait a spell," he said and turned his glance on the Hagemans.

Bill was helping Julie from the buggy. She

25

popped open her parasol to hold back the sun, then walked into the store. But she paused in the doorway and looked across at Cord. Bill Hageman saw this and I knew good and well that he didn't like it. He stepped under the hitch rail and crossed over with the rolling walk of a man who has spent a lifetime on a horse. He was as tall as Cord, but his hair was light, and his complexion always seemed sunburned. He had a bland sort of face, the kind a man liked to have if he wanted to play good poker. Consequently it wasn't always easy to tell how Bill felt about things, and this irked Cord, who liked a broad understandability in everyone.

There were a few people around Ponca City who figured that Bill Hageman had a poke of money, seeing as how he rarely spent a nickel. He had been wearing the same patched canvas brush-jacket for six or seven years, and his jeans had been patched so many times that they looked like one of those clown suits. All he needed was different colored cloth to make them funny. I don't think Bill ever owned a suit of clothes.| And his hat must have been his father's for it was one of those high-crowned, wide-brimmed Texas hats, a long time out of style.

Bill wasn't very old, near thirty, which was Cord's age, but he moved slow most of the time, drawled when he talked, and acted like a man forty and then some. He stepped around the end of the watering trough and stopped with one run-over boot planted on the edge of Lanahan's porch. Bill's fingers brought out his sack tobacco and he rolled a cigarette, keeping his hat brim tipped down so that it cast a shadow over his face. When he arced the match he looked up at Cord.

"Big day finally arrive?"

"Seems like it," Cord said. "The world treating you all right, Bill?"

"You'll never hear me complain," Hageman said easily. He looked at me and a smile flitted briefly over his thin lips. "I don't see much of you, Smoke. Got a mad on?"

"No," I said. "Been pretty busy. We're figuring to ship in a week."

Maybe I shouldn't have said that: Cord gave me an irritated look; he was a man who liked to keep O'Dare business among the O'Dares.

Bill Hageman's eyes mirrored a momentary interest. "Didn't know you'd completed a gather, Cord. I may come over and cut the herd. Likely some of my stuff has drifted."

"I haven't seen any of it," Cord said. "If any turns up, I'll have Smoke drive it across the river."

"You don't have to go to the trouble," Bill said. "I'm shipping a few head myself. Maybe I'll drop over in a day or two." He snubbed out his cigarette and turned his head toward the depot as the train whistle sounded again, closer this time. "Buy you a drink, Cord?"

"Not now, thanks," Cord said. He turned his head and watched as Hageman went into Lanahan's, and when the doors stopped swinging, he turned to the horses. We mounted and rode slowly toward the depot. Cord was watching the front of Herschammer's store and as he drew abreast, Julie Hageman stepped out as if by accident. Only I knew better. Women never did anything by accident where Cord O'Dare was concerned.

She pretended pleasant surprise and I felt a quick resentment; never have I been able to accept pretense in a woman as something cute. Cord nudged me heavily and I remembered my manners; quickly I swept off my hat. This irritated me even more because if I hadn't been thinking about what was going on between them, I'd have remembered without reminding.

Julie looked at me, her eyes bright in that way women's eyes are when they talk to one person and are only conscious of another. "I haven't seen you in over a month, Smoke. Have you forgotten the way across the river?"

"No," I said. "A lot of things have needed doing." I pulled my eyes away from hers for fear she'd read something there I didn't want her to read.

Cord said, "We'd best get along, Smoke. Train's about due."

This was all the excuse Julie needed. Her eyes

switched to Cord and she gave him a smile. "Tonight you'll have another woman in the house. Do you mind if I drop over to meet her?"

"You're always welcome," Cord said. "We don't see enough of you, Julie."

He kneed his horse around and we rode on. When she was out of earshot, I said, "You don't get along with Bill but you shine up to his sister. That don't make sense."

He looked at me in that careful way he had. "Go easy now, Smoke. I guess it's been four or five years since I've belted you for talkin' out of turn." Then he smiled and the edge of the threat was dulled. "I guess you like her, huh?"

"Some," I hedged.

"Julie's got nothing to do with Bill," he said. "Or what I think about him."

"And what do you think?" I asked. "You pace around each other like you was walking on eggs."

"I'll wait until I'm sure, then I'll say," Cord said.

2

One thing you want to understand about Cord is that when he'd had his say about something, all talk ended, and further questions just made him mad. Which is why I let the subject of Bill Hageman drop; Cord would bring it up again when the notion struck him.

We pulled the buggy in on the shady side of the depot. Ma and Luther were around in front on the cinder platform. We dismounted and went around the building to join them. Ma stood under the faded passenger awning while Luther walked along the right of way, looking up the track and sweating. He carried a handkerchief in his hand and frequently mopped his face.

Cord said, "Can I get you some water, Ma? It's hot as blue blazes."

"I'm all right," Ma said softly. She looked at him and smiled and reached up to brush at the lock of hair hanging over his forehead. "You're right thoughtful, Cord."

I could see the train coming now, black smoke rolling from the bulged funnel stack. And I could hear the sounds of wheels clacking over rail joints and finally the rattle of couplings as the engineer applied his brakes. The engineer whistled again when he approached the grade crossing just outside of town, then the train huffed into the depot, slid past with a hiss and a sigh, exhausting steam and the flavors of hot oil. We never rated much of a train at Ponca City, just a baggage car, one passenger coach, and a couple of freights, but we regarded it with the same amount of respect that city folks lavished on the Katy *Flyer*, or the Texas-Pacific *Gen. Sam Houston*.

The conductor was first out, with his little steps, and we sort of moved away from the depot and stood in the full sunlight. A man got down, a drummer with a heavy suitcase and a thirst that couldn't hardly wait. Then Heck Overland, who hung on at Rindo's Springs long after the town had all but died out. Heck glanced our way, nodded briefly, then went to the shade to stand. He was an odd man, near friendless, and he seemed to like it that way. I'd been to Rindo's Springs a few times with Cord, and other than an occasional grunt, Heck Overland wouldn't even speak to me.

Two more men filed out of the coach; I'd never seen either before. They gave the depot a quick survey, then headed for the main drag and Lanahan's Saloon.

Finally she stepped down; I was afraid she never would. Luther, like a danged fool, whipped out the tintype, studied it to make sure his eyes weren't playing tricks on him, then ran up and grabbed her. She dropped her canvas satchels—I guess Luther scared the daylights out of her—then she recognized him and threw her arms around his neck. Yes, I said recognized, because Luther rode all the way to Guthrie so he could have a picture taken to send to her.

Ma and Cord and I all crowded in and started to talk at once, but Ma's soft cooing sort of pushed all our babble aside. "So you're Edna. My, my, but ain't you a pretty thing." She had her fat arms around Edna and was leading her to the shade. "Get her grips, Smoke."

I grabbed them and followed around the corner of the depot. Luther was moving about, trying to get a word in edgewise, but Ma was doing all the talking, trying to tell Edna Shore everything there was to know in the first minute, the way women do when they get together. Edna was doing as much talking as Ma, and this was something that's always amazed me, how two women can both talk at the same time and still understand each other.

Edna was sure a lot younger than I figured. Eighteen, I guessed, or maybe nineteen, but surely not the twenty-one she claimed to be in her letters. She was a small girl. Came up to my chin if she stood straight. Her face was kind of heart-shaped, and she had brown hair, parted in the center and braided down the back. I don't suppose she'd ever take a beauty prize but she was still a looker, the kind that wouldn't fade out after a summer's sun had got in its licks.

But right there, at the neck, that simple, homespun girl ended. Now I never claimed to be up on the latest fashions, and until I was twenty-nine, I never saw a town larger than Guthrie, which, as I recall, had about forty-eight hundred population, but I sure knew that Edna Shore had been twice around the park in different buggies. Her dress was a tight fit, and most men would agree that there was enough there to fit tightly. She had taken some of the fancywork off because I could see where the stitches had been, and a few odd ends of thread remained. But her clothes were garish enough to make any man look twice.

Luther didn't notice, and Ma wouldn't have known a high-stepper if she'd have seen one, and Cord didn't care. So I figured I ought to keep my opinions to myself, and did.

Edna's eyes kept moving from Ma to Luther, then to Cord, and when I stepped up, they moved to me. I don't know what I expected. Probably hard eyes filled with cynicism, but they weren't that way at all. They were warm and compassionate, and sorry for a lot of undefined things, the kind of eyes some people have who try to do right and never seem to have any of it come out. She smiled, and it wasn't the kind of a smile she handed out to just anyone; this was for me, special. And then I knew I was going to like her in spite of the things I'd thought. I was even a little ashamed for thinking them in the first place.

"You're Smoke, aren't you? Luther's mentioned you many times."

Isn't it hell what a pretty girl's smile will do to a man's poise? I suddenly had an extra foot, a fool's expression, and fingers that just couldn't hold my hat. I dropped it, then bumped her when I stooped to pick it up.

Luther cleared his throat and said, "Ma, I guess there's nothin' to be gained by standin' here." He looked at Edna Shore, then got red in the face. "If the sight of us O'Dares ain't scared you into changin' your mind, I expect we'd best get on to the church."

"I like the O'Dares," Edna said, taking Luther's arm. "And I haven't changed my mind about anything."

He let out a ringing whoop and before anyone could stop him, lifted Edna and plopped her onto the rear seat of the buggy. The fact that we owned a family rig in the first place needs a little explaining. It wasn't that we were buggy-riding people by a long shot, but Ma was so consarned heavy that we could never keep springs in the top buggy, so Cord went to Omaha and bought a canopy-top surrey.

Luther got in beside Edna, and I handed up the satchels, then tied Luther's horse on behind. Cord was already mounted and I helped Ma in as I always did. The rig kind of sighed when she settled herself; as soon as I swung up we drove down the street.

The Baptist Church was on the corner of Peace and Railroad Streets and we pulled up in front. Cord got down and helped Ma while I tied the team. Reverend Elder came out of the parsonage, shrugging into his coat. He was a bean-pole man with whiskers and a voice that could thunder when he got the feeling about some particular sinner. His eyes were deep-set and piercing, and now and then I'd have sworn he was singling me out during one of his sermons, and those eyes could make a brave man hunch down in his pew and wish he'd behaved himself.

But the Reverend was smiling now and ushered us into the church. Some people would take a look at our church and say that they'd seen hay barns that looked better, and likely they had. But we liked the church, probably because there wasn't a man, woman or child big enough to carry a bucket of nails who hadn't helped build it. And for that reason the place seemed a little more godly than something that was bigger and maybe a little fancier.

As usual, Cord had made all the arrangements ahead of time, and although I'd never attended a wedding before, I expected it to come off without a hitch; things usually did when Cord had his say.

Luther and Edna stood before Reverend Elder

and Luther kept squirming as though his collar was choking him to death. I knew it was impolite, but I kept watching Edna's face; I couldn't help it because I never saw a woman look exactly like that before. Sort of like she was in a dream, but| a dream where everything came true and she didn't know whether to laugh or cry about it.

The Reverend was talking, but I wasn't listening. Marrying didn't take as long as I thought it would; somehow the permanence of marriage fostered the idea in my mind that the procedure was involved. Finally Reverend Elder said, "The ring, Luther. You have a ring?"

I never saw Luther panic quite that badly before. His face drained of color and he looked at Cord, as though this were all his fault, since he was supposed to have arranged everything. Cord looked blank, then shrugged while Luther floundered in a sea of embarrassment. Then Ma was pushing around Cord and me, her fingers digging into her cloth reticule. She came up with a plain gold band that Pa had placed on her finger thirty years before. She handed it to Luther.

Cord's eyebrows pulled into a frown and he said, "That's yours, Ma."

"Take it," Ma said, trying to press it into Luther's hand.

Edna's eyes got real filmy and tears settled along the bottom lids. "I just couldn't," she said.

"But it's the kindest thing anyone ever did for me."

"I want you to wear it," Ma said in that way she had when she didn't want a lot of sass or argument. "It's what I always planned for the first girl my sons took for a wife."

Luther took the ring then and lifted Edna's hand. Reverend Elder smiled and clasped his bony hands together and the whole thing was over, just like that. Luther smothered Edna in his arms and kissed her and we all laughed because he seemed very embarrassed. Cord put his hand on Luther's shoulder and kind of moved him back. "Here now," he said easily. "You got the rest of your life for that, and this is the only chance I'll ever get. After all, if it wasn't for me, you'd never got acquainted with her in the first place."

I didn't see much wrong with the idea of Cord kissing his bride, but the way Cord sort of swooped her to him left me with the uneasy feeling that the wrong man had married her. Leastways he didn't give her a peck on the cheek. His arms imprisoned her for a long moment and she didn't fight him either. When he released her, Edna just looked at him, her eyes kind of wide and surprised, and a little hurt. About what I wouldn't know.

Then Luther and Cord were pushing me and I braced my feet like a balky calf touched for the first time by a rope. This only made things worse and to get it over with, I gave Edna a quick peck on the cheek. This caused Luther and Cord to howl and my face must have been red enough to satisfy them. Only Edna wasn't laughing. She looked at me steadily, then put both hands on my face and kissed me smack on the lips. She said, "I like you, Smoke."

Ma saved me from making a consarned fool of myself. She put her big arm around Edna and hugged her. Cord gave the Reverend a five-dollar gold piece and we all went outside to the buggy. This time Ma got in the back and Luther and his new wife rode in front, Luther driving. I untied Luther's horse and mounted. Cord said, "You go on, Ma. We'll catch up." He turned his head and looked uptown. "Bill Hageman offered me a drink. Think I'll take him up on it, among other things."

I couldn't see anything out of the way in what he said, but Ma did; she gave him a straight look. "You do whatever you think best, Cord." She raised a hand and patted her beads. "When you see a snake, I guess you just got to step on it."

Luther pulled away, taking the road home, and Cord and I turned toward the main drag. "What did Ma mean, Cord?"

He seemed preoccupied and I wondered if I hadn't asked something I shouldn't have. Cord could be plenty short with a man when he wanted to be. Finally he said, "A man never has trouble unless he lets the little things grow."

That's all he would say about it. We tied up at Lanahan's and went in. The three farmers who had been sitting with Lige Bingham and Vince Randolf had gone out and Bill Hageman was now at their table. He stopped talking when Cord and I stepped inside, and he watched us carefully as we crossed to the bar.

No beer this time; Cord ordered from the best bottle Lanahan had. I sagged against the bar, shot glass cradled between my palms. Cord picked up his drink and turned, looking squarely at Bill Hageman and the two farmers with him.

Observing Bill and Cord together, I couldn't help comparing them to a couple of blooded fighting dogs, each staying in his own back yard, yet always subtly daring the other to step across the line, just once. Trouble lay between these two men and for as long as I could remember, it threatened to boil over. They always seemed to walk the narrow ledge, yet neither had taken the one step over. The reason for this dislike was a clouded thing; I didn't understand it and I often wondered whether they did either. They both acted as though they possessed some knowledge of the other that precluded any possibility of trust or understanding.

Cord downed his drink and said, "You say you're shipping too, Bill? Pretty good year?"

On Hageman's face there was the clear intention of not answering. But he changed his mind and said, "No profit in cattle any more."

"I guess not," Cord said easily. "I hear that the Indians have been thinning out your herd pretty bad."

"I've lost a few," Bill Hageman admitted. "You?"

"The usual," Cord said. "It's hard to make a decent gather any more, with the Indians eating my beef." He turned to Lanahan, who stood quietly behind the bar. The other men in the saloon were listening. "Fill this up again, Pete."

"Sure." Lanahan uncorked the bottle. "Smoke's too?"

"One's enough for Smoke," Cord said, then turned back to Bill Hageman, glass in hand. "How many are you shipping this year?"

Hageman didn't want to say, that was plain enough, but he couldn't duck so straight a question. "Eight hundred head."

"Well," Cord said, eyebrow raised. "That's a goodly number. Leaves you pretty thin, don't it?"

"I'm going to give the graze a rest for a year or so," Bill said flatly. "Anything wrong with that?"

"No, not if you can afford it," Cord said. He turned the glass slowly in his hand. "You know, Bill, those Indians are plenty smart. Seems that they only run off the young stuff, and always before a man can clap a brand on 'em. That ever strike you as peculiar?"

"What are you getting at, Cord?"

"Nothing much," Cord admitted. "But I've been around Indians all my life and they're generally pretty stupid when it comes to stealing something. All of which leads me to believe we're blaming the wrong coon for robbin' the henhouse."

Bill Hageman looked at Bingham and Randolf, then placed his hands flat on the table top. "Meaning?"

Cord shrugged and tossed off his drink. "I mean, we're being rustled blind. We ought to take a look around, Bill."

"If you think rustlers are working this part of the country, then call in a marshal from Oklahoma City," Hageman said. "I trust my neighbors, Cord."

"Sure you do. All I said was that we ought to look around a little closer." Cord paused as though rolling words around in his mind. Then he came out with it; I didn't think he would. "Just because a man's a neighbor, that don't make him honest."

Bill Hageman had already guessed what Cord was going to say because he kicked back his chair and was on his feet before Cord finished the sentence. Vince Randolf grabbed Bill's arm hard enough to tear the sleeve clean out of his jacket, but that didn't stop Bill one danged bit. He would have jumped the distance between him and Cord if it hadn't been for the .44.

Cord's hand whipped back to his hip, brushing his coat aside. In one movement that swivel holster was turned and the barrel of the gun pointed squarely at Bill Hageman's belt buckle. Now I don't suppose there was a man in Lanahan's Saloon foolish enough to think that Cord couldn't hit such a target, but there was some mental speculation as to whether he would or not. I stood there with my mouth open, watching Bill. He stood like a tree. His eyes were polished glass.

Pete Lanahan spoke. "Cord, you wouldn't shoot him!"

"I don't like to be jumped," Cord said. He still kept the .44 pointed at Bill Hageman.

Hageman's breathing was heavy, like he had run a far piece and knew the race wasn't over. "I never carry a gun, Cord." He had trouble saying it, as though anger choked him nearly speechless.

"Maybe you ought to," Cord said softly. "You know, a man as jumpy as you can get himself into real shooting trouble."

"You accused me of something," Hageman said flatly. "Do you expect me to stand here and take it?"

"I didn't accuse you of a damned thing," Cord

said. "What I said could have been meant for Randolf, only you took it personal. You feel guilty about something, Bill?"

Hageman's face drained completely of color and he began to tremble. Carefully he raised his hands and shucked out of his brush jumper, flinging it on the floor. We could all see that he hadn't lied; he didn't have a gun. "Cord," he said, "you'd better shoot me now because I'm going to take that gun away from you."

When he jumped, it was like a cat jumps, one bound, and I stepped back so as not to get tangled in this. Cord was backed against the bar and I thought sure that Bill Hageman's charge was going to drive both of them clean through it, but at the last instant Cord stepped aside and Hageman came against the bar hard enough to move it four inches and bring down a shower of whiskey glasses. There was a moment when Hageman was spread facedown and Cord balled his fist, flailing Bill across the back of the neck, driving his face into the polished cherrywood. Blood spouted from Bill's nose, then Cord stepped back, quickly unbuckling his gunbelt.

"Here," he said, not even looking at me. "Catch."

I caught it and stood there stupidly while Bill Hageman pivoted and made for Cord. There was a lot of fight in Bill Hageman; I have to give him credit for that. He wasn't scared of Cord and he was willing to carry the fight all the way, which might be the reason he had so little advantage. Cord took a raking fist on the neck and belted Bill heavily in the mouth, splitting his lips. Hageman bellowed like a gored bull and tried to ram Cord, head down, but Cord moved aside, clubbing Bill in the face and throat.

Probably every man in Lanahan's that day was as convinced as I was that the fight was pretty one-sided. Cord knew how to hurt a man and he did a bang-up job on Bill Hageman. Most men would have tried for a quick put-down and let it go at that, but Cord had other ideas. He kept stunning Bill with short jabs, never hard enough to knock him down, but sharp enough to cut him up mighty bad. Of course Bill was getting in his licks, but he lacked the steam, or couldn't get in a solid punch that did any good.

Cord had closed Bill's left eye and was working on the right, now that he had smashed Bill's lips and broken his nose. Bill was pretty near blind, but like I said, he had a lot of heart and wasn't scared. Any other man would have faked a fall and quit the fight then and there, but Bill Hageman seemed determined to stand as long as he could.

The whole thing was making me a little sick and even Pete Lanahan, who had seen more than his share of drag-down fights, voiced a protest: "He's had enough, Cord!"

But Cord acted as though he hadn't even heard Lanahan. He slammed his fists into Bill's face; the sound reminded me of a butcher flinging a quarter of beef on a clean block. Hageman's knees were beginning to wilt. When he finally fell I was glad. Cord stepped back, breathing heavily through his open mouth. He walked over to the bar, stepping over Bill Hageman to do it. Uncorking a bottle, Cord poured whiskey over his torn knuckles, then leaned against the bar. His bottom lip was bleeding, as was a cut over his eye, but he didn't care about these things.

I gave him back his gun and he put it on, all the time looking at Hageman, who was never completely unconscious, but too badly beaten to even get to his hands and knees.

"Smoke, take him to the horse trough and clean him up." I stared at Cord, wondering why he should even care. He made an impatient gesture with his hand. "Go on, do as you're told now."

Vince Randolf and Lige Bingham had not left their places. They watched as I put my hands under Bill's armpits and with a little grunting staggered outside with him. The news of the fight had spread; exactly how always remained a mystery with me as no one had left Lanahan's place since it had started. A dozen of Ponca City's citizens were stomping down the boardwalk as I got Bill around the hitch rail and on the edge of the trough. The water wasn't what I'd choose to wash with, but this wasn't the time to get fussy. I let Bill down as easy as I could, but he slipped and fell in.

One of the men laughed and I looked at him. "You think that was funny?" I asked. You may wonder about my taking Bill's side this way, but I ought to explain about me, if you haven't already guessed it: I like everybody; that's my failing. Don't have an enemy in the world.

But now that I'd mentioned it, the man standing there didn't think it was so funny after all and he wiped the grin off quick enough and just watched.

Bill Hageman was sputtering and trying to sit up now. I took off his neckerchief and bathed his face. Cord had made a real mess of it and Bill was going to wear a few scars as a reminder for the rest of his life. His eyes were beginning to focus and he looked at me. All he saw was that I was an O'Dare and he knocked my hands away from him. At another time this would have made me sore, but not then. I stood there and waited and when he began to sag again, I helped him sit up. He knew he couldn't make it alone and he said, "Will you help me, Smoke?"

Now I figure it takes a pretty big man to put his feelings aside like that, so I hoisted him to his feet and we started across the street to Julie's buggy. The crowd followed, as they always do, but I paid them little mind. Bill couldn't do anything but lay down so I helped him settle in the back of the rig. He threw an arm across his face to keep off the sun.

I turned around and looked at everyone in general. "Ain't you people got business some-place else?"

Sam Buckner, who ran the feed store, squinted at me. "You O'Dares is gettin' pretty pecky, ain't you, Smoke?"

"You'd better drift, Sam," I said, and meant it. Normally I don't pick fights, but I'm capable of handling those that come my way.

For a minute I thought Sam was going to try me for size, but finally he scratched his head and said, "Hell, where's the profit? You fight one O'Dare and you got to fight 'em all. Too hot for that." He turned and pushed his way through and others followed him until I was alone by the buggy.

Not alone exactly, for Julie came out of the Bon Marche, saw the crowd breaking up and came on with a quickened step. By the time she was near enough to see Bill stretched out, she just let go of her parcels and parasol and ran toward him. She looked at her brother and then at me and the glance she gave me was meant to kill me as dead as could be. There wasn't anything I could say; the best thing was to leave her alone and give her time to figure out it wasn't my fault. So I went along the walk and gathered up the things she'd dropped and placed them in the buggy.

She was angry. As angry as I'd ever seen her, but she no longer pointed her anger at me. "Smoke," she said with frightening quietness, "just give me one good reason why this happened."

"Argument," I said, being purposely vague. "Honest, Julie, there wasn't anything I could do. They just lit into each other."

"I've been praying this would never happen," she said. Then she looked past me, toward Lanahan's, and from the way her expression hardened, I knew that Cord had stepped out.

Now some men would have walked a wide berth around Julie until she cooled off, but Cord wasn't built that way. He untied our horses and led them across the street. When I looked at him his face was expressionless and if he was a bit sorry for what he had done, then he sure wasn't showing any of it to either of us.

Julie faced him squarely. "You gave me your promise that there wouldn't be trouble. Is this all your word's worth, Cord?"

"You knew this had to happen," he said.

"If I was a man I'd shoot you," Julie Hageman said evenly.

Cord smiled faintly. He stood with his head tipped forward, the lock of hair bobbing slightly. His eyes held Julie's, as though there were so many secrets between them that a little thing like his beating up her brother wasn't going to destroy them. He spoke so softly that I almost didn't catch his words.

"Would you, Julie? Would you really shoot me?"

He didn't wait for an answer; I guess he knew it, and I could guess close enough. He just stepped around his horse and swung up. There wasn't anything I could do but to follow. Julie stood by the back of the buggy, her eyes never leaving Cord's face.

I said, "I'm sure sorry, Julie."

I doubt that she even heard me. Cord rode out and I sided him and at the end of the street I looked back in time to see Julie turn to her brother.

For a time Cord and I rode without speaking. The mid-morning sun was scalding and I pulled my hat low to cut the mounting glare. After a while Cord paused to roll a smoke. I said, "You really think Bill Hageman's a rustler, Cord?"

"Someone is," he said. "Cattle don't just disappear, Smoke."

"Hell, Vince Randolf could . . ."

"Vince don't have the guts," Cord said quickly. He puffed on the cigarette. "Figure it out for yourself, Smoke. A calf is weaned, then disappears. No brand, nothing to identify him." He paused to scan the vast stretch of flats. "There's a hundred gullies out there, Smoke. Gullies where a man could hold a few head for a week or so without there being one chance in a hundred of their being found."

"But where would the rustler sell 'em?"

He looked at me, kind of squinty-eyed. "One of these days I think I'll take a ride up to Rindo's Springs and have a talk with Heck Overland. There may be some shipping going on there that we don't know about."

"You think Bill's . . ."

"I ain't thinking a thing," Cord said evenly. "When I know for sure, then I'll do something permanent about it." He grinned at me. "You make light of what happened in Lanahan's in case Ma should ask you, you understand?"

"Sure, Cord. Anything you say."

He laughed then and rapped me on the shoulder with his fist. "Come on, let's get home. We got a new woman in the house, and she ain't at all hard to look at." He jabbed his horse with his heels and rode ahead of me, letting me eat his dust; only with a brother like Cord, I didn't mind.

3

I suddenly felt a little better about what had happened in Pete Lanahan's Saloon, and a little guilty for even thinking that Cord would ever pick a fight without a good reason. A man ought to have more faith in his own blood kin, but I guess Cord understood me well enough. Surely a lot better than I understood him.

When we got on the home place, I took the horses to the barn and gave them a good rubdown with clean straw. Cord went on to the house. When I was finished, I cut across the yard and, danged if I know why, used the front door instead of the back. Luther and Edna were sitting on the horsehair sofa with the stereopticon and a bunch of cards strewn around, but they had given that up for kissing. They broke away quickly when I closed the door.

" 'Scuse me," I said and didn't fool either of them.

Ma heard me and came down the hall. "Smoke, for land's sake, can't you see they want to be alone?" She took me by the arm as though I was six years old and marched me into the kitchen, now heavy with the flavors of peach pie. "You want something to eat?"

This was a needless question because I never passed up food. Cord was finishing a plate of eggs and some cold meat. He winked at me when I sat down and I knew there would be no questions from Ma about the fracas in town. Cord had handled this in his own way, as only he could handle it.

I don't recall Ma ever being as gay as she was the rest of that day. We didn't do much work, just hung around the house. Toward mid-afternoon Luther took Edna for a ride in the buggy to show her part of the ranch. They headed toward the river and the cottonwood groves down there and it was nearly dark before they came back. I was by the barn when they drove into the yard. Edna got down and went on to the house while Luther put up the team. Cord came out and walked to the barn. I saw him speak to Luther but was too far away to hear what he said. Cord laughed and Luther got pretty sore, but by the time he walked across the yard he was over it.

Julie came across the river, which surprised me, considering how the day had turned out. Ma came out as she dismounted by the porch, a smile splitting the melon plumpness of her cheeks. "My, my, you brought something," she said, noticing the bundle under Julie's arm.

"Yes," Julie said. "It's a quilt my mother made for me. I'd like Edna to have it."

"Hardly blanket weather," I said and Ma shot me a look that said to shut my mouth.

This seemed to fluster Julie, then I realized too late that this was all she had to give, and my big mouth had made it pretty apparent. Ma took Julie's arm and led her inside. "Cord's around someplace," she said. "Go fetch him, Smoke. He'll like to see Julie."

I went as far as the porch, then stopped. Danged if I was going to make a match there, even though Ma had her heart set on it. After a decent interval of time had passed, I skirted the house and entered by the back door.

Edna and Luther were seated around the table; Julie sat across from them and Ma was bringing coffee from the stove. She saw me and said, "Get a cup for yourself."

"It's so flat here," Edna was saying. "But I like it. The air smells so clean and fresh."

"Different from Chicago," Julie said. "Of course, I was only there once. My mother is buried there."

"Couldn't you find Cord?" Ma asked.

I looked at her quickly, trying to think of a suitable lie that she wouldn't immediately see through. Julie glanced up and knew instantly that I hadn't even looked for him. "Didn't see him in the yard," I said. "You want me to look again I'll . . ."

"Oh, drink your coffee," Ma said. "Land's sake,

you're blind in one eye and can't see out of the other."

"I really have to be going," Julie said, rising. When she said her good-byes and made her promises to visit again, I edged out the door and was waiting by her horse when she walked up.

Very softly she said, "You're a poor liar, Smoke. You didn't look for Cord."

"You gave me the idea you didn't want to see him," I said.

"Perhaps I didn't," she said and stepped into the saddle. "Smoke, Edna's nice. I like her."

"Going to take some getting used to," I said.

"We all have to make our adjustments, Smoke. Give her a chance. Will you promise me that?"

"Sure, but what . . ."

"A woman gets lonely out here, Smoke. Believe me, she'll need help from time to time."

"All right," I said. "But come back, huh?"

"Do you think I'll always be welcome?"

"With me? Yes."

"Too bad others can't be like you, Smoke."

With that she wheeled around and rode back toward the river. I watched her for a time, then went back into the house.

That night the kitchen table groaned under the weight of Ma's cooking, and I ate too much of everything. With the sun gone, a cool breeze came up, scuffing dust along the flats. Cord went to the front porch to sit with Ma while Luther and

Edna went to the parlor. This kind of made me extra baggage and I walked to the horse corral to look at a new foal.

I couldn't help thinking of Julie Hageman because she was always in my mind, one way or another. But now I had a good reason for thinking of her and the more I thought, the stronger grew the desire to see her again. Sounds pretty silly, don't it? Especially after her recent visit. But we hadn't talked about the things that really needed talk. Just three miles across the river she was sitting alone with her trouble and because I was an O'Dare, I couldn't deny the responsibility for my part in it.

Ma and Cord were around the other side of the house and Luther was so wrapped up in Edna that he wouldn't know if a twister blew in from Kansas. Figuring that I could sneak out without them knowing it, I quietly saddled up and led my horse out of the yard. When I'd put enough distance between myself and the house, I stepped into the saddle and rode toward the river.

This was the part of our property I liked the best. I knew every rabbit warren among the rushes lining both banks, and when I was a lot younger, I used to spend considerable time there, exploring all the cavelike openings in the brush. A man could cross most any place, for the river bottom was fairly solid and the water was no higher than a pony's belly. I splashed across and struck outfor the distant ranch buildings, and in less than an hour, I came into Bill Hageman's yard to dismount by the porch.

There was a light in the bunkhouse and a lot of light in the main parlor. One of Hageman's crew came out of the bunkhouse and looked across the dark yard, but trouble wasn't common around here so he went back inside. I stepped onto the porch. The front door was open and I could hear Julie's quick step inside. I knocked and a moment later she came down the hall. When she saw who it was she pushed the screen door open, then stood aside.

"I guess I shouldn't be here," I said, "but we never got around to talking about Bill."

"He's asleep, finally," Julie said. "Come on in, Smoke."

I took off my hat and followed her down the hall. Now I know it's the custom for Eastern folks to invite visitors into the parlor, and usually that room is reserved for just that, but out here where neighbors are less formal, we always use the kitchen. And that's where Julie took me.

Wherever you go, there's coffee, and she poured a cup for me, then sat down at the table, facing me. The kerosene lamp cast shadows on her face, and bright highlights where the light hit her squarely. I drank my coffee, not knowing what to say, which is pretty stupid since I came over just to talk. But then I never did have much to explain to Julie. She was smart and understood more than she let on.

"You don't like trouble, do you, Smoke?"

"No, I don't."

"But you're not afraid," Julie said. "Yet you were sorry this happened. Why did it happen, Smoke? I have a right to know."

She was right. She did have an explanation coming, but I didn't have one for her. Still, she was Julie and for such a long time I'd dreamed of doing anything she asked; the answers came easy. "Cord thinks someone's rustling cattle."

She looked at me, real surprised. "He can't think Bill . . ." She gave a short laugh of disbelief. "Did he accuse Bill of that?"

"Bill took it that way."

"Smoke, you don't believe that!"

"Gosh, Julie, I don't know what to believe! Anyway, it didn't make much difference. I couldn't butt in after they started to fight."

"I understand that," she said quickly. "Smoke, if Cord believes that Bill is a cattle rustler, then he believes wrong. You know Bill and you know he wouldn't steal from anyone. Why, we've lost cattle too!"

"He said he was resting his graze for a year or two," I mentioned.

Julie snorted through her nose. "A proud man's way of prolonging the admission that he's about licked. Another year of this dry weather and there won't be a blade of grass standing." She rubbed her hands together and her eyes reflected the deep trouble she endured. "Bill's sold most everything off, Smoke. He has no choice. We've simply got to weather out two tough years or we're lost."

I thought what a great pity it was that I lacked the words to tell her how much I wanted to help. But she must have understood for she reached across the table and put her hand over mine. I set the coffee cup down so I wouldn't drop it. That's how weak she could make me feel.

"You're a good friend, Smoke. And I haven't thanked you for helping Bill."

"You don't need to do that," I said.

"That's right," she said, smiling. "You don't do things for the thanks, but just because they're right and you'd have a hard time doing anything that wasn't decent." She wiped her hands over her eyes as if she were tired and sleep was no help at all. "What's going to happen to us, Smoke? Are we going to end up fighting each other?"

"I wouldn't ever do that, Julie."

"You're an O'Dare," she said, "and you'd side with your family. That's your way, Smoke. And I wouldn't want to see you any other way. But we don't dare to fight. Can't Cord see that? Bingham and Randolf want to irrigate the land across the river. So do Higgins and Mooney and Everett on your side. Bill's tried to be friendly toward them but they're hard men to understand; they don't trust us." She got up and poured a cup of coffee for herself. "Smoke, we've got to patch this up between Cord and Bill."

"How?"

"I don't know, Smoke, but we have to. I can't do it alone. Will you help me?"

Would I help her? I'd been waiting a long time for her to ask, and now that she had, I could only nod like the village idiot. Finally I found my voice. "Sure, Julie, if you think that's the answer."

"I think it's the only answer," she said. "Smoke, Cord may be right about the rustlers, but he's wrong about Bill. We know the Indians are not wholly to blame, although they get their share. For a long time Bill's thought it might be the farmers; after all, we surround them, and other than a few fences their fields are unprotected and cattle drift where they please. I'm grabbing at straws, Smoke. I know Bill and I know Cord. The next thing they'll start shooting at each other. And Bill can shoot if he has to."

That thought had never occurred to me, but now that she had mentioned it, a small worry was born. Although I'd never seen Bill Hageman packing a pistol, I knew that he had one hanging in the hallway, and it was too well worn not to have been used daily for a good many years.

I guess every man tries his hand at six-gun handling. I sure did when I was younger and had the foolish notion that when I got fast enough I could run away and be a U. S. Marshal like Bud Ledbetter. But that was in the past and I hadn't even picked up a short gun in four or five years.

"I'll talk to Cord," I said, then realized how that sounded; a little ridiculous, like I was promising to beard the bear in his den. "He'll listen, Julie. I'll make him sit and listen."

"Then tell him Bill will be over in three or four days. As soon as he's able to ride."

"You're coming too, ain't you?" I just wanted her around where I could sit and look at her.

"Yes," she said. "I'll come too."

Overstaying my welcome was never one of my faults so I got up and went to the front door. Julie walked with me. We stood on the dark porch and listened to the wind whisking softly across the distance. On impulse, I said, "There's the Grange dance coming up a week come Thursday. I'd be obliged if I could take you."

"Why, Smoke!" Then she laughed. "Yes, I'd really like that."

This was a time when being casual was a real effort and I nearly flung my hat into the air and did a jig. But I held myself in real well and said good night as polite and casual as you please. She stood on the porch while I rode back toward the home place, only I was in no hurry, now that I could look forward to a week from Thursday.

After crossing the river I dismounted, tied the horse, and lay back beneath the cottonwoods and tried to figure out how I could be so blamed lucky. As many a time as I'd wanted to ask Julie to go someplace with me, my nerve always gave out at the last minute, but tonight it had held as firm as you please.

Being in no hurry to get home, and knowing no one would worry about me, I stayed along the river until after midnight. One thing about us O'Dares, we always came and went as we pleased and no one ever bombarded us with a lot of questions later. If I felt like going away for a few days when the work was light, I'd just do it, not saying where I was going, when I was coming back, or where I'd been when I got back. For being a close family, we had a habit of minding our own business, which was probably the reason we didn't fight among ourselves.

When I did get home, the place was as quiet as a graveyard. I turned my pony into his stall and hung up saddle and bridle before walking to the house. I was on the porch before I realized someone was sitting there and I jumped a foot.

Edna said, "I didn't mean to scare you, Smoke. A girl?"

"Thought you'd be in bed," I said, taking a seat on the porch railing.

"I'm too happy to sleep," she said. "I'm afraid that if I did sleep I'd wake up and find that it was all a dream." The rocker creaked slightly as she shifted. "Have you been across the river?"

"Yes," I said.

"That trouble Cord had in town, wasn't it with the people across the river?"

I knew what she was getting at, and because she was new, I let her get away with it. "That was Cord's trouble," I told her. "They ain't mad at me. And I guess the trouble will pass in time."

"Your brother likes to have his own way, doesn't he?"

"Luther?"

"No, Cord."

"He runs things," I said. "Ever since Pa died, Cord's been the boss. We ain't suffered any."

"Yes, I can see that. He's a strong man, Smoke. I knew that the first time I ever saw him, in Chicago." She looked at me; her face was a vague oval in the night light. "I liked him, Smoke. I suppose a lot of girls have liked Cord O'Dare."

"He's been around the park once or twice," I said, then added, "So've you."

That hurt her feelings, and I hadn't meant to do that. "Does it show that much?" she asked. She bent forward in the chair, her face close to mine. "Smoke, this is a new life for me. Give me a chance to live it."

"I wouldn't do anything to hurt you," I said. "Only Luther's pretty dumb about a lot of things."

"And you're not? That seems odd, Smoke. He's older than you."

"Age don't have anything to do with it," I said.

"Edna, when Luther started to write to you, I thought he was loco. Seemed an odd way to court a girl. Well, he's married you now, and I guess you got a right to make something of it. Luther's been kind of a homebody; Cord's kept a tight rein on him. I wouldn't want to see him taken advantage of just because he's green."

"I think I understand," Edna said. "And Smoke, you'll never have to worry."

"Who's worrying?"

The talk was at an end; she got up and stepped to the door.

"Smoke, is your girl nice?"

"She ain't exactly my girl," I was sorry to admit.

"But is she nice?" Then Edna shrugged. "It really doesn't matter, Smoke. Good night."

4

After she went into the house, I sat alone on the porch and wondered if I hadn't shot my mouth off again when I should have kept my opinions to myself. My judgment of her had been sudden and unkind, and she deserved better than that. Finally I got up and went into the room I had shared with Luther, only now I had it to myself; Luther and Edna had moved into the back room which was always kept as a spare in case we had overnight company. The place seemed a little bare now that Luther's things had been moved. I took off my suit and hung it in the closet, then lay down on the bed.

My concern about Edna breaking up the O'Dare family was not as strong as it had once been, and although she was still a stranger, I decided that I would do my best to understand her. Her being a city girl naturally aroused my suspicion, and that was wrong; I had no right to judge her from my brief observations of Omaha's night life. Of course Edna would have a lot to learn, and so would I, especially about her clothes and why she liked them so loud. And I'd have to get used to the powder she wore on her face. Time,

I told myself; that's what it would take. We'd both need some time.

The next morning all of us began to learn a few more things about Edna. Nothing from what she said, and I guess nothing too important, but when Ma asked her to help with the breakfast we soon found out that she'd never spent much time in a kitchen. Cord seemed vastly amused and Luther was apologizing all over the place which made things worse, for it drew attention to that which she wished we'd ignore. Edna seemed about ready to burst into tears and I guess she would have if it hadn't been for Ma, who could smooth anything over when she put her mind to it. She gave Edna an easy job, watching the bacon so that it didn't burn, and even then some of it did. But Luther grabbed all those pieces and ate them as though that was the way he liked bacon.

"I'm sorry," Edna kept saying in a desperate voice. "I'll do better."

"Well, never you mind," Ma said. "My lands, didn't your folks ever teach you to cook?"

"I—I lived a lot with relatives."

"She had things fixed for her," Cord said. "Servants and all. Ain't that right, Edna?"

I knew good and well that she didn't and wondered why Cord said such a thing, or put her on the spot like that. Edna looked at him and tried to make up her mind whether to dispute him or not. Ma said, "You never mentioned relatives in your letters, child."

"Well," Cord said, "Edna never had real relatives, did you, Edna? Just Aunt Harriet, but she wasn't Edna's real aunt, was she, Edna?"

"No," Edna said in a small voice. "Can't we drop it, please?"

"We're all one family," Cord said. "We don't keep secrets from each other."

Edna raised her head and stared at him for a long moment. Even Luther's attention sharpened. Cord waited, his eyes steady on hers, then Edna put her head down and began eating.

The meal turned a little stiff; Cord and Edna ate in silence, and Luther sat there wondering what the devil was going on. Ma tried her best to get everyone off on the right foot, but she ended up by doing all the talking. For myself, I could only wonder, and I really didn't want to do that, for a man is led into some wrong conclusions that way.

Since I had things to do, I excused myself and went to the barn to saddle my horse. Before I could leave, Cord came out, his fingers making a cigarette as he crossed the yard. He had on his .44 so I figured he was going to town.

"I could use some help today," I said. True enough we didn't have enough stock to make this a full-time three-handed ranch, but I was getting tired of all the heavy work falling on me.

66

"Get Luther," he said. "I'll be back by noon."

"What's to do in town now that we didn't do yesterday?"

He looked levelly at me and said, "You wouldn't pry into a man's business now, would you, Smoke?" He got his horse out of the stall and smoothed on the saddle blanket. While he saddled, he said, "I want you to look over the herd we're going to ship and see that they haven't busted down Wade Everett's fence. There's some grass near his spring that the critters yearn for."

"Sure," I said.

Some folks I know would have said that I shouldn't have taken all the bossing around that Cord handed out, or keep on doing a share of the work that was properly his, but I really didn't mind. You never minded doing for a man like Cord because he knew how to treat a man to get the most out of him. And then there were those times when he had given me his most. I can't rightly put my finger on one of them for you, but when I'd get balky, Cord would quietly remind me that when I was just a shaver, he'd done plenty for me.

So that's how I ended up doing the work Cord should have done.

Since we made our gather a week or two before, we'd been holding the herd near Wade Everett's place; he was one of those farmers surrounded by O'Dare land. Not having the money to fence properly or build a holding pasture, we had to make the land work for us, and near Wade Everett's place was an old dry wash that ran for better than two miles, steep-sided, and butting up to the fence he had built. We always drove our stock in from the east end where the wash began, then let them drift until they came to the fence. Pretty good grass there, and a spring. So unless a dirty summer twister came up to spook them, the herd would stay around that wash for a month or so.

A half-hour ride brought me to the wash and I rode along the rim. Everett's place was ahead, a small sod shanty and a barn only half finished. The walls were up but the roof was only bare poles and rafter beams. I could see Everett's kids playing in the yard, three small boys who didn't have a decent pair of jeans to their name. Everett was working on his barn and he looked steadily at me, not answering my wave. I just couldn't get close to the man somehow; none of us could. His wife didn't show herself either. I guess she shared her husband's distrust for cattlemen.

I spent most of the day moving the herd away from Wade Everett's fence. In a day or two the cattle would wander back toward the spring and I'd have this to do all over again, but like I said, when you're too broke to fence, then you have to make do with what you have.

Cord had returned from town by the time I arrived at the home place; his horse was standing three-footed by the porch. I took my pony to the barn and then crossed the yard. As I stepped onto the back porch I could hear Ma talking in the kitchen, laughing and telling Cord how wonderful he was, as if he didn't know it already.

Everyone was standing around the kitchen table when I came in. Edna and Ma were laughing, but there wasn't much pleasure in Luther's expression. Cord stood to one side with his cigarette dribbling ribbons of smoke past his face. The presents he'd brought home were on the table amid a blizzard of wrapping paper. Ma had a music box, the kind that holds face powder and all the knickknacks that women like to fuss with. Pretty fancy, I thought, with all the carving and gilt paint to make it look like gold. Ma had the lid open and the danged thing played some waltz in a tinkling voice, and when it ran down she wound it with a key and listened to it again.

Edna was admiring herself in a hand mirror. Cord had bought her a toilet set: brushes, comb and mirror, all inlaid with pearl. Mighty pretty but I couldn't help wondering how much it had cost, the price of a roll of fence wire anyway.

"That was the sweetest thing," Edna said. Turning to Cord, she put her hand lightly on his cheek and then stood on tiptoe to kiss him on the lips.

Luther frowned but said nothing; he was always very sensitive. Ma was too blamed wrapped up in the music box to notice the way Edna looked at Cord. "I'll put these away," Edna said and started to leave the kitchen.

"You're a hard woman to buy for," Cord said.

Edna turned and looked at him, sort of expectant, as though she was sure she was going to like what he had to say, but wanted to give him a chance to say it. "Why, Cord?"

"I'll be switched if I could think of anything good enough for you," he said. "So I bought the mirror and you can look at your pretty self."

"How sweet," Edna said and hurried out of the kitchen.

Luther shifted his feet and tried to find proper words. "It's my place to buy her things," he said. "And I would if you'd stop sittin' on all the money, Cord."

Taking the cigarette from his mouth, Cord looked surprised and a little hurt. "You ain't jealous, are you?"

"What if I am? She's my wife. I'll do for her."

"Well, sure, if that's the way you feel about it," Cord said. "Hell, I bought Ma a present. I didn't think it'd look right if I didn't get Edna something."

"Now, boys," Ma said firmly, "let's not argue. Luther, you know your brother wouldn't do anything to hurt your feelings or make you feel belittled, would you, Cord?"

"That's right, Ma. You like the music box?"

"It's the prettiest thing," she said. "Cord, you're so thoughtful I don't rightly know what I'll do with all the pretties you've bought me." She wound the key again and then stood there with her head tipped to one side, nodding to the waltz.

"I'll get you other pretties," Cord said. "Nothing's too good for you, Ma. You're my best girl."

"Pshaw!" She laughed and her eyes were like diamonds, many-faceted, reflecting her deep pleasure. "You'll up and marry one of these days, then where'll I be?"

"I'd never do that; you know that, Ma." I was surprised at the seriousness in Cord's voice. "You're all I ever want, Ma. I mean that."

"Of course you do," Ma said. "And I'm beholden to you, Cord. Your old ma couldn't have asked for a better son."

This kind of talk always bothered me, as though they were lovers or something, each sworn to some secret pact. I went out on the back porch to stand and a moment later Luther came out. He glanced at me and said, "You get sick of hearin' about how good he is after a while." He stomped across the yard and went into the barn. A short time later he rode out. Cord came to the door in time to see this.

"Where's he going?"

"I didn't ask and he didn't say." That was a pretty short answer for me to be giving Cord, but he must have had other things on his mind because he let it pass.

"Luther goes away a lot. I'll have to ask him about it one of these days." He looked at me. "The gather all right?"

"They'll hold until shipping time," I said. "Did you make any arrangement for the cars?"

"That's what I went to town for. Did you go over to Hageman's last night?"

"Yeah."

"Stay away from there," he said.

The way he said it, short and not to be disobeyed, riled me. "That an order, sir?"

He looked at me, sharp-eyed and steady. "Better not get sassy, Smoke. You've got no business over there. There's some doubt in my mind as to how clean Bill Hageman is. If it turns out that he's been rustling our stock, then I wouldn't want you to get mixed in it."

"I didn't go there to see Bill," I said.

For a moment he teetered between amusement and laughter, and laughter won. "Well now, ain't you the little rooster? I always thought Julie liked her men full grown."

Nothing, it seems, sets one man against another as quick as a woman; I was ready to launch into something I wasn't big enough to win. "You mean your size?"

"Well, since you said it, I guess that's what I meant," Cord admitted. He looked at me careful-like. "It occurs to me that you might have asked her to go to the Grange dance with you."

"I did! And she's going!"

"Now that's sure sweet," Cord said. "Likely she said yes because I haven't asked her yet." He paused, and I waited, knowing that something was coming; it always did after one of those pauses. "You think you're a real he-cat now, don't you?"

"I never claimed nothing like that. What are you trying to make out of this, Cord?"

"Nothing, nothing, boy. I'm just trying to set you straight so you don't get hurt over something. Some men fool themselves about women, and you're one of 'em. A man's got to face what he is, Smoke. Understand himself. Stay in the place God made for him. Now you're second rate, Smoke. Always have been and always will be. That don't make you any less likeable, but I wouldn't want to see you getting hurt over Julie. I guess she'd be amused enough with you until a man came along."

"You're a cockeyed liar!"

I thought he was going to hit me; he did the last time I called him that. But he let it pass; Cord had generous moods. "Smoke, a man ought to back his opinion, especially of himself. You willing to gamble a little?"

"Name it."

"Well, you go ahead and take Julie to the dance, but to show you how fickle a woman can be, I'll just bet you a dollar that I take her home."

Oh, that Cord was a smart one. He boxed me neat all right. I wouldn't have defended myself and he knew it, but I'd defend Julie Hageman until I was blue in the face. "You got a damn bet!" I snapped.

"You're mad now," Cord said gently. "But I'm doing you a favor. All for you, and someday you'll thank me for it."

"For me, hell! You just like to rut around women!"

The pleasure vanished from his eyes so quickly I could hardly believe it, and his voice held a sharp-edged chill. "Now you know that's a lie, boy. And I want you to tell me it's a lie." He waited while I tried to pull together enough nerve to buck him. "Go on, tell me." He put his hand on my shoulder and dug in his fingers. "You're a long way from grown up and you've got to learn to quit flappin' your mouth. Now I'm waiting."

"I guess I didn't mean it," I said and the fingers relaxed their pressure. I wheeled and stalked to the barn, cussing myself and Cord and anything else that got in my way. How can I explain? To say that he just plain scared me sometimes wouldn't be the whole truth. Or to say that I gave

74

in all the time because he was my older brother and about all the father I remembered wouldn't be the truth either. I was some scared of him and some in awe of him, and a lot beholden to him, and I wondered if I'd ever get completely away from him. Some-times I thought to myself that if I didn't, I'd never be my own man. I'd end up like Luther, so halter broke that he couldn't sneeze unless Cord said it was all right. Or maybe I'd end up married like Luther, to a woman Cord had picked. Or like Ma, so blinded that she thought of Cord as kin to God.

I never entertained these thoughts about Cord unless he got me good and mad, and then I could pick him apart without mercy. Looking back, I can see that those were the only times when I ever saw Cord with any degree of clarity. But afterward I was always sure that it was I who was mistaken, and the picture I had created was warped by my own unreasonable anger.

5

Always before, I could work off a good mad in one day, but this one clung like beggar lice. The first day I dug post holes until my back was fit to break, getting ready for that fence we would someday be able to afford. The second day I cleaned out the barn and repaired the roof, replacing sod patches that had been lifted off by last summer's twisters. Cord didn't turn a lick to help and I took a savage pleasure in doing it all alone. I say alone because Luther was always riding off toward the river with Edna. They'd stay all day and come back just in time to set down to the supper table.

The third day was spent near Wade Everett's place, rebunching the herd we meant to ship. I dragged in around dusk and when Ma called me for supper, I had half a mind not to answer. But the other half told me that I would only make things worse, for Cord would come out and get me, giving me a public lecture on sulking, which I wasn't in the mood to take.

Ma had the table set and Edna was placing the platters of food. Luther came into the kitchen, freshly scrubbed; he sat down immediately. I was at the sink cleaning up when Cord came in. He looked at Luther and asked, "When are you going to get that river bank explored?"

"Aw, shut up," Luther said.

Edna stood by her chair and then Cord smiled and pulled it back for her, adjusting it when she sat down. Luther looked around in time to see this and his face flushed darkly for he should have performed that small courtesy instead of Cord.

Edna didn't look at her husband and this embarrassed Luther even further. By the time Luther thought to pick up Edna's plate and serve her, Cord was already doing it. He gave her dainty portions and handed it back. Ma sat down, looked at the dabs of potatoes, greens and small bits of meat, then said, "My, that ain't enough to stuff a canary bird, Edna." She heaped her own plate and began using knife and fork together, mixing peas with gravy to keep them on her knife.

There was little talk at first, then Cord asked, "You like it here, Edna?"

The question startled her, I think; she looked as though she were afraid of him. "Yes, it's wonderful. There's so much room. Miles of it."

"Nothing like Chicago," Cord agreed. "Think you'll ever be homesick? I mean, Aunt Harriet might miss you, Edna."

"No," Edna said quickly. "I—don't think she'll miss me." She seemed confused and embarrassed and kept her attention on her plate.

"Well, you might just want to go back someday," Cord said. "For a visit." Luther looked up and stopped eating. Cord smiled and added, "Luther'd get a kick out of meeting Aunt Harriet."

She seemed desperate, and maybe a little trapped. Her glance went quickly to Luther, as though she expected help. "You wouldn't like my aunt," she said. "Honestly, she's difficult to get along with."

"Aw," Cord said, "Luther might take to her right away. Of course he ain't much for leaving the home place, but once or twice a year I go East to see firsthand how the market's doing. Might take you both along the next time."

"I'd like that," Luther said.

An uneasy silence fell and we waited for Edna to speak, but she tipped her head forward and stared at her plate. Ma said, "Now let's eat before everything gets cold."

Throughout the meal Cord kept waiting on Edna. Little things like seeing that she got the nicest slice of meat, or pouring her coffee for her. Stuff like that. Luther didn't like it, but there wasn't much he could do about it without making himself out a damned fool.

Ma kept up a bright, covering chatter and I kept my mouth shut.

That is, until there was a lull. "Cord," I said, "Bill Hageman's coming over to talk to you in a day or so."

He stopped with his fork half raised. "What about?"

"About the quarrel you and him had. Julie thinks it ought to be patched up."

"You been back over there since I talked to you?"

"No," I said. "We talked about it the last time I was there."

"We?"

I'd put my foot in it without thinking, but I decided to play it bold. "Yes," I said. "I guess we can understand why you spoke a little hard to Bill in town; everyone's been pecked about the stock that turns up missing. But there's others in this beside cattlemen, Cord. The farmers are just waiting until you and Bill start fighting, then they'll dig ditches and put up more fences to make a road. When the fight's over, they'll have the river drained down a foot and a half, and a way across your property."

"I think I can handle the farmers," Cord said. "Smoke, don't try to run my business."

"Wasn't trying to!" I snapped. "Cord, it's going to look mighty bad if you and Bill Hageman don't get together and talk. It'll look like you've got something to hide, or else are trying to put the blame on him."

"Could be it belongs there," Cord said.

"And could be it don't," I said.

"Well," Luther said, dryly, "that was quite a speech, Smoke. I wish I'd made it."

Cord gave him a darted glance of irritation, then said, "All right, Smoke, how will it look bad?"

"This whole thing is heading for something that only a U. S. Marshal ought to handle," I said. "And a marshal would take a long, careful look at anyone who didn't do his damnedest to keep trouble from coming to a head."

Cord took a minute to think this over, and my argument must have had some effect, for he said, "All right, I'll talk to Bill, but that's all I'll promise to do."

"As long as there's no more fighting," I said.

"All right!" Cord shouted. "I said I'd talk to him, didn't I? What do you want me to do, apologize?"

"You don't have to get riled," I told him. "Hell, Cord, I just don't see what's to be gained if you and Bill ram heads. The way you rode him down the other day folks will get the idea you're trying to run the whole country."

"Maybe I could," Cord said. "Go on, finish your supper. We'll settle this when Bill comes over."

This was, I knew, about as good as I could expect to do, and I was satisfied with it. Cord was a stubborn cuss when he got his neck bowed, and it never paid a man to push him too hard. I finished my coffee, excused myself and went outside. The sun was going down nice and slow, shooting the last hot rays across the prairie. When it dropped completely out of sight, the night came on fast, and soon after, the cool wind began to blow.

With shipping day coming up, Luther and Cord went into the parlor to work on the books. We always worked pretty close to the red side of the ledger on the home place. That is, since the Territory was opened up and we had to start all over. That sell-off the government made us pull nearly drove us under, and I guess Cord never forgave them for it. One thing you have to understand about the cattle business is that we can't move in a hurry. Takes at least two years to move the stock, since they're strange critters who like to get used to a piece of land before they live on it. If you move them to new graze in the fall, they'll die off during the winter because they're not familiar with the cover. The government gave us thirty days' notice to move and a marshal came around to make sure we didn't take thirty-one. They couldn't have picked a worse time of the year and we had to sell off to a man who knew we were in a bind and gave us next to nothing for the stock.

Yet I always figured that we were lucky, since we cleared something, which was more than most of the cattlemen did. Bill Hageman, and two outfits thirty miles to the south, were the only ones, besides ourselves, who managed to land on their feet. But when I say cleared even, remember that I'm discounting ten years of hard work.

Cord managed to hold over enough to buy a few hundred head and since we'd lived pretty low on the hog, we made a go of it. With money being mighty scarce, I always worried a little when Cord came home with some gimcrack for Ma. Not that I resented her having something to make her happy, but those danged things cost money, and I didn't have to be told how tight things were pinching.

Cord had plenty of reason to be a driving man, and I would be the last to blame him for getting his hackles up every time a calf turned up missing. "Rustler" had gotten to be a foul word around Ponca City and Bill Hageman was hurt as bad as we were, only he wasn't as quick to let his temper out as Cord was.

The back door opened and Edna came out. She smoothed her dress and sat beside me on the steps, her arms wrapped around her raised knees. "The nights are nice," she said. "It stays hot in Chicago. The buildings block out the breeze unless you live on the lake shore."

"Where did Aunt Harriet live?"

"Not on the lake shore," Edna said softly.

"Where then?"

"You wouldn't know the place if I told you," Edna said. She suddenly put her hand on mine. "Smoke, let me forget, will you?"

"Sure, if that's what you came here to do."

She bit her lip for a moment. "You don't like me, do you?"

"This may surprise you," I said, "but I do. That's a fact, Edna. I think you're going to be good for Luther. But why ain't you honest with me?"

"I am," she said. "Smoke, I've never pretended with you, or Luther. Whatever I was once, I didn't want to be. And I hoped I wouldn't always have to go on, living from day to day. Now I don't have to hope any more, do I? I'm Luther's wife, and I have a real family. Could anyone ask for more?"

"Sometimes I think about lightin' out on my own," I confessed. "A man gets to wonderin' if he could make it or not."

"We all think like that," Edna said. "But it's no fun being alone, Smoke. You don't know what the bottom's like unless you hit it once." She laughed softly and stood up, brushing off the back of her dress. "But that's in the past now. Why look back when it only makes you sad?"

She went into the house and closed the screen door. I heard Ma come into the kitchen, then she stepped to the door. "What are you sitting there for, Smoke? Land's sake, ain't you the moody one." She went back into the hall and then I heard Luther's step. He said something to Ma that I didn't catch, then came on outside.

"If you knew a lick about arithmetic," he said, "you could be adding figures instead of me." He sat down and stretched his legs. "Damn little profit this year. Eating money is about all."

"Bill Hageman's thinning out to rest his grass," I told him. "Julie says there won't be any grass left if it don't rain."

Luther shook his head. "Don't see how Bill can afford to let his land lie." He looked at me quickly. "I get irked at Cord, but damn it, if he wasn't pinchin' the money like he does, we'd be on chitt'lin's and beans. Beats me how he can make a dollar stretch so." He fell silent for a minute. "You and Edna been talkin'?"

"Some," I admitted.

"She'll take some gettin' used to," Luther said. "A quiet girl. But I guess it's better than having one whose jaws are going from morning to night. You spoke up pretty bold tonight, Smoke. Don't you like the way Cord runs things around here?"

"Not all the time. You don't either."

Luther shrugged. "Smoke, I've learned to keep my mouth shut. You better do the same. When a family gets to arguing amongst themselves, there isn't much left." He laughed softly and slapped me on the shoulder. "You want to take it easy, Smoke. You go at a thing too sudden and Cord don't like it."

"We got a right to dislike something when we want to," I said.

He laughed. "Good night, hothead." He got up and went inside.

After a while I got bored, just sitting there, so I walked to the barn to check the horses and have a look at the foal. I toyed with the idea of saddling up and riding over to see Julie, then decided that I'd better not. She'd think I was overdoing it a little, and I'd always been a little worried that I'd wear out my welcome there.

Cord and Ma were sitting on the porch in their rockers when I recrossed the yard. Every night they sat that way. As I crossed the porch, they said a brief good night. That was always the same, too, as though they wanted to make sure the little flock was bedded down and tucked in, and peace reigned over their domain.

Surely there must have been people in the world who would have welcomed this concern and attention, but it irritated me, and I didn't understand why it should.

6

The next morning Luther and I had an early breakfast and rode out to the herd. They had drifted a little toward Wade Everett's place and we drove them back again. Everett was working on his barn and he watched us all the time we were near his fence. I waved at him but he ignored it.

Luther said, "What the hell's the matter with that man?" He turned his horse and when I went to follow, he said, "Stay here."

He rode around to the end of the fence, bent down and unhooked the gate, then rode onto Everett's property. Everett came down from his lofty perch and stood in his yard as Luther rode up. By edging close to the fence, I could hear what they said.

"Don't you have the common decency to acknowledge a man's wave when he's trying to be friendly?" Luther asked.

"I was busy," Everett said flatly. "And I'm busy now; you're wasting my time."

The kids gathered by the soddy door and Mrs. Everett stuck her head out. Even at sixty yards I could make out her frightened expression. Luther was getting down off his horse. "God damn you,

Everett," he said. "You just don't want to get along, do you?"

"I don't start trouble," Everett said flatly, "which is more'n can be said for the O'Dares."

I cupped my hands around my mouth and yelled, "Let's go, Luther!"

He didn't even look at me, just waved his hand as if to tell me to go home. Everett was backing up, one step at a time, and Luther was stalking him.

"I got a gun," Everett said loudly. "Don't make me use it!"

"You wouldn't use it," Luther said and jumped him.

"Ma!" Everett yelled, and then he was bowled over by Luther's fist. I'd seen enough. I backed my pony away from the fence, raked him with the spurs and charged, clearing by a comfortable margin. Luther had Wade Everett on the ground and was whacking him in the face. Everett's woman was screaming at the kids and trying to cock the hammer on the big trap-door Springfield .45-70.

There wasn't time for me to dismount and drag Luther off so I shook out my rope and after whipping a wide loop in it, made an underhand cast, beneath the pony's neck. My throw was good and as soon as the rope settled, the pony backed off to tighten it. Luther let out an enraged bleat, then I dragged him flat on his back for fifteen yards. He got up, wild-mad and spitting dust, so I sat him down again. I did this three times before he cooled off enough to understand that the fight was over. Everett had raced to the soddy, grabbed the .45-70 from his wife and gave us both a clear look down the barrel.

"Now you get the hell off my property! By God, git and don't come back!"

Luther's face was as white as a curd and I wasn't sure which way his anger was directed, at me or at Wade Everett. Anyway he didn't want to argue with a five-hundred grain bullet. He mounted and wheeled out of the yard and I followed him, glad to do it.

As we rode toward the home place I thought Luther was never going to speak to me again, but after a time he calmed down enough to talk. "I suppose I ought to thank you, Smoke. Everett's woman was all set to shoot me."

"You pulled a damn fool stunt," I said.

"Don't rub my face in it!" He blew out a gusty breath. "I was going to show myself that I could be as tough as Cord. It didn't turn out that way."

"You better say nothing about this to Cord," I suggested.

"I suppose," Luther said. "Thanks, Smoke. There'd have been real trouble if you hadn't roped me like you did."

We said nothing more about it and rode on. By the time we arrived, Bill Hageman and Julie were already on the front porch. Ma was coming out with a pot of coffee and Edna followed her with a tray of cookies. Cord was in his rocking chair, and after putting up the horses, Luther and I walked over.

Cord took one look at Luther's dirty clothes and asked, "What happened to you?"

"I tried one of Smoke's underhand roping tricks and tripped the horse," Luther said. He passed quickly into the house, brushing past Edna and Ma before Cord could launch a comment. I looked at Bill Hageman. There sure wasn't any love passing back and forth between him and Cord. Yet they hadn't gotten around to muttering threats at each other, which was a good sign. Bill's face was a mess if I ever saw one. One eye tight shut and the other puffed to an inefficient slit. His lips were out of shape and so thick he could hardly talk straight.

Ma smoothed out the strained atmosphere by passing around cups of coffee and by the time everyone had a cup in one hand and cookies in the other, they discovered that there were no fists left to shake in each other's faces. Julie smiled at me, which made my day all right, then she moved aside to speak to Edna. Julie said a lot of nice things, about how pretty she looked and how glad she was to have her for a neighbor. But Cord was frowning and wanting to get on with business.

Cord was peculiar that way; once he fought with a man, he didn't want to have anything to do with him afterward. Now I say that once it's over, forget it. A fight isn't something on which to establish a hate; it's a way of clearing one up.

"What have you got on your mind?" Cord asked, looking at Bill Hageman.

The rest of us quieted down. Bill sat on the porch rail, holding to his habitual silence. "It seems," he said, "that we had a set-to over something I didn't rightly understand at the time."

"I understood it," Cord said. "And I guess you did too because I mentioned no names, yet you took it personal as hell."

"Sounded to me like you were accusing me of rustling," Bill said.

"What I said was, because a man's a neighbor, that don't make him honest. Randolf is a neighbor. So's Bingham. I meant to include 'em all."

The way it sounded to me, Cord was asking Bill Hageman to shoulder all the responsibility for the fight, and Bill proved that he was up to it when he said, "I guess then I jumped off the handle. My mistake, Cord."

"I figured that," Cord said, not showing an inch of give.

"I'm as tired of being rustled as you are," Bill said. "We were both touchy as hell, half suspecting each other. But I think it's high time we got some sense and started to work together.

There are things we can do without jumping down each other's throats." He paused, as he often did when speaking, as though he were putting words together in his mind and trying them out to see how they'd sound. "I was hoping we could figure out some-thing, Cord."

"I agree to that," Cord said, looking off at the flatlands, his eyelids pulled together. "We've been here a long time. We both started from scratch and did all right until the damned government kicked us off. They broke our backs and there wasn't a damn thing we could do about it."

"Best forget that," Bill suggested. "Thinking over something that can't be fixed will sour a man."

"Sour?" Cord looked at him. "Damned right I'm sour. Since the farmers came here we've been breaking our backs trying to get back on our feet again. When I lose a calf it's profit from my pocket. Profit I need bad. If I ever catch a man running off my stock, I'll take a rope from my saddle and stretch his neck."

This drew a deep frown on Bill Hageman's forehead. I think it was a frown. It was difficult to tell, so distorted was his face. "We've got laws, Cord. Let's send to Oklahoma City for a U. S. Marshal and let him investigate this in a proper way."

Cord's head came around quickly and he stared at Bill Hageman. "You damn fool, do you want to lose what little we now have? How much do you own legally? The two sections you and Julie drew? The rest you got the same way I did, squeezing the farmers when they couldn't take any more." He blew out his breath and rolled a cigarette. "A marshal is the last thing we want around here, Bill. He'd do more than investigate. He'd file a report with the land office in Oklahoma City and we'd lose everything. End up with a grubby potato patch without enough water to grow anything." He wiped his hand across his mouth. "In another five years it won't matter; we'll be entrenched too solid to move out. But now we're hanging on by our fingers. Ain't you got sense enough to see that?"

"Yes, I see it," Bill said. "But I could go back to two sections. I could if I had to. The land don't mean that much to me, Cord."

"Well, it means something to me," Cord told him quick enough. "I'm not going to spend the rest of my life raising blooded bulls on four hundred acres or running dairy cattle. It took me nearly ten years to build the first time and then I lost it. It's not going to take me ten years to build again."

"There's no quick way," Bill Hageman said. "I'd like one, as much as you would, but there isn't any way. Let's send for the marshal, Cord, and take our chances that he won't notice the shaky deeds we hold."

"No! I'd rather handle it alone first. You want to help, fine. If you don't, then it's all the same to me."

"You mean, hang the man if you catch him?"

"As high as I can throw my rope," Cord promised.

Bill didn't like this talk. Neither did I. He looked at me, and then at Cord. Finally he put his glance on me again. "Where do you stand in this, Smoke?"

Cord answered for me. "He stands with the O'Dares. Just where he's always stood."

Bill Hageman sighed and shook his head. He was through arguing; we all knew it. "Sorry you feel that way about this, Cord. Of course, I'll have to be against you should you try to shove anything resembling private law down anyone's throat."

"You suit yourself," Cord said. "You've always cottoned to Vince Randolf and the others."

"They're free men," Bill said, "and they have rights. I wouldn't stand by and watch them lose any of them, Cord."

"That's putting it plain enough," Cord said, standing up.

The visiting was over. I moved back, stepping off the porch so I could help Julie mount her horse, but like always, Cord was ahead of me. So I stood there and watched him do what I wanted to do, and I watched Julie's face. She wasn't much different from the other women I'd seen around Cord. She disliked him for the things he believed, yet she felt a strong compulsion toward him, as though he had a magnetism that pushed aside all else, leaving only the core of his manhood as an attraction.

Julie smiled when he held her stirrup and blushed a little when he put a hand on her thigh to steady her up. Bill was mounted and impatient to leave. Julie held that smile as she turned to join him, and a short distance from the house she pivoted in the saddle to wave, not at me, but at Cord, who still stood there like he knew what was coming and was waiting for it to happen.

He finally came back to the porch. His glance touched mine and I think it would have been better if he had said, "I told you so," or anything to clear the air. Only he was never the kind to rub something in although I knew now that I'd be owing him a dollar come Thursday.

At a time like that, a fellow can hate pretty easy, and Julie Hageman was high on the list, for I felt betrayed, used, and pretty worthless, made so by a woman who could be as fickle as she was pretty. I couldn't hate Cord, not because I owed him so much, but because he couldn't help being irresistible to women. Behind that handsomeness lay a threat of brutality, a sense of power now restrained, a danger disguised; all this had an effect on women and I'd seen some fairly levelheaded ones make fools of themselves because of what they saw in Cord, or thought they saw.

Luther was still in the house, but Ma was waiting on the porch. She said, "There'll be trouble now, Cord."

He laughed. "No more than we already have. Not enough money."

"You'll manage," she said. "You've been a good manager, Cord."

"I want to do more than that. I want a lot more, Ma."

"Whatever you think best, son," she said and went into the house. That was her final answer; it never varied. Whatever Cord thought best. Whatever he did, that was all right with Ma. And if it turned out wrong, Cord would bring her a new pocketbook or a shell comb and then the mistake was never mentioned.

Luther chose that time to come out and Cord looked sharply at him. "Where were you?"

"In the house. I heard it all."

"Then the next time, show yourself," Cord said. Luther made as if to walk past Cord and was taken by the arm and jerked around for his trouble. "Listen to me! I'm telling you some-thing!"

"Hell, I hear you," Luther snapped and jerked away. He stalked across the yard to the barn and

I followed him a moment later. He was in the tack shed, going over his saddle.

"What are you so mad about?" I asked.

"Leave me alone, Smoke."

"Hell, I just asked."

"And I just told you!" He threw the saddle aside and stood up. "Damn it, one O'Dare telling me what to do is enough. Don't you start too."

"If you don't like what's going on," I suggested, "then open your mouth. You don't have any trouble telling me about it."

"I sure as hell noticed that you went along with what Cord said. Don't preach to me about what I do. Clean out your own outhouse before you tell me mine smells."

"You don't have to take out your grouch on me," I said.

"Then don't ride me! Damn, you'd think after a man was married he'd come into some rights around here." He pawed his mouth out of shape and looked around as though he were looking for something to smash. "If I had twenty dollars of my own, I'd take her and ride out and never come back."

Since I'd heard him say that before, I didn't take it too seriously. "I got twenty I'll loan you," I said, meaning it as a joke.

Only Luther sure didn't take it that way. Before I knew what had happened he'd balled his fist, popped me on the jaw and the next thing I knew

I was sitting on the dirt floor and looking at him through a shower of bright lights and hearing some far-off bells ringing.

I knew by his expression that he was sorry he had done that, but like most things begun in anger, this got out of hand in a hurry. I got to my feet a little quicker than he thought I could and drove a stiff one into his stomach. He went back against the cobbler's bench and I laced him across the mouth, drawing blood.

When he came erect I was waiting and for a minute we locked together, sawing back and forth, bumping into things, knocking them every which way. This must have set up quite a racket because it brought Cord and Ma from the house on the run.

The next thing I knew, the shed door banged open and Cord had us each by the collar and was knocking our heads together. I pushed at him and yelled and he finally stopped, but held onto us. Ma came in, blowing hard from her run.

"What the hell do you think you're doing?" Cord asked.

Ma's hands were fluttering and her face was wrinkled like she was going to cry. "Fighting. Oh, my goodness, just look at you. Just look."

Cord gave me a shake. "Smoke, I asked you something."

"Just an argument," I said, then looked at Luther. "Sorry."

He stared as though he couldn't make up his mind whether or not to let this pass. Then he said, "Me too, Smoke. Did I hurt you?"

Actually it was the other way around. I had a nice bruise on my jaw but Luther had two choice cuts on his face, both bleeding a little. Then he laughed and wiped the back of his hand across them and Cord let us go. He turned and took Ma's arm and walked back to the house with her.

Luther waited until they were both out of earshot, then said, "I don't know what got into me, Smoke. Just had to hit something."

"Yeah," I said. "I guess you did."

Luther picked up his saddle from the floor and went to the stall for his horse. There was no reason for me to hang around, but I did. When he was mounted and ready to leave, I asked, "Where'll I say you've gone?"

He pursed his lips for a moment. "Out." He lifted his reins. "And I can't say when I'll be back. I may ride over to Rindo's Springs and see Heck Overland."

I watched him ride out in the direction of Wade Everett's place, then went to the house. Cord was in the parlor reading a month-old magazine and Edna was in her room; I could hear her moving about as I went into the kitchen. As usual, Ma was baking something for supper.

She looked at me quickly and said, "You

shouldn't fight with your brother, Smoke. Haven't I taught you to hold your temper?"

"It wasn't anything," I said.

"When two brothers try to bloody each other," she said, "it's usually something. Was that Luther that just rode out?"

"Yep."

"He's a restless boy. I wish he was steadier, like Cord." She gave me a smile. "You're a restless boy too, Smoke. You yearn a lot. What for, I'll never know. As long as we have each other, we have everything."

"I guess, Ma."

7

The kitchen was hot and I went out to stand on the back porch. I could see the fringe of cotton-woods along the river, and as I watched, I saw a horseman emerge from the trees. As he came on, I recognized Julie Hageman's pony long before I could make out her exact features. This struck me as odd, that she should be coming back. I left the porch and walked out into the yard, meeting her. The legs of her jeans were nearly dry, which meant she hadn't crossed the river and then come back.

She pulled to a halt and stepped down. Sweat was bright on her face and had soaked her white shirtwaist around the shoulders. "Smoke, is Cord at home?"

I should have known she hadn't come back to see me. "Yeah," I said and led the way to the house. She tied her pony at the porch and I held the door open for her. Ma came out of the kitchen to see who it was; she seemed surprised. Cord lifted his head when we came into the parlor, then he put his magazine aside and stood up, smiling. "I didn't expect this pleasure," he said. "Can't I get you something, Julie?"

"No thank you," she said. "I didn't go home, Cord. I had to come back and talk to you."

"Well, I'm sure glad you did," he said, taking her arm. He gave me a look that bade me find somewhere else to stand, but I didn't budge an inch. I stood in the archway while Julie sat down.

"Cord, it was hard for Bill to say what he meant. And you didn't make it any easier for him."

"A man does what he thinks best," Cord said. "Do you mean to say it for him?"

"Perhaps," Julie said. "I want you to come with me, Cord. To go around to Vince Randolf and Wade Everett and all the others. I want you to leave your gun at home and talk nice to them. I think it's important that you make friends with the farmers, or at least try to."

Cord frowned. "You're asking a lot of me, Julie. These people might take friendship for weakness."

"That's a chance you'll have to take," she said. "Please, Cord. Do this much for me."

"Well, I'd do a lot for you, Julie, but this, I don't know. I was figuring to go to town today. Couldn't we make it some other time?"

"There may not be much more time," she said. "Cord, what I'm asking is fair."

"Fair to Bingham and Randolf and Everett, but not fair to me." He paused as though considering this. "Julie, when I lose a calf I can't help but wonder if it hasn't gone on one of the farmers' tables. Was they to rile me a bit, I might suggest that to their faces."

"You won't go then?"

"I can't," he said finally. "Sorry, Julie. Anything else but that. Cattle and farmers don't mix. They wouldn't listen to me."

"Is this your final answer, Cord?"

"It has to be. Now if you'll excuse me?" He went to his desk and picked up his gunbelt. After buckling it on, he put on his hat. "You're pretty, Julie. One of these days I'm going to have to tell you how pretty."

He edged past me and went out to the barn. Julie sat in the chair, her hands idly brushing the arms. There was defeat in her voice. "I tried, Smoke. I thought he liked me enough to do it."

"Cord keeps his likes separate from his wants," I said, sort of letting it out before I thought.

She looked at me sharply. "What are you trying to say, Smoke?"

"Not trying to say anything," I assured her. I wished she'd stop looking at me that way, as though she were measuring me for something.

"Smoke, did you ever do anything that Cord didn't want done?"

"Sometimes. And I've been whaled proper for it."

Cord rode out and Julie and I remained quiet

until the sound of his horse faded. The house was silent except for Edna moving about in her room and Ma humming in the kitchen. She had the music box going and was humming the waltz.

Julie left the chair and came close to me, so she wouldn't have to talk so loud, I guess. "Smoke, would you go with me? Would you speak for Cord?"

The idea left me a little numb; I'd crossed Cord before, but never like this. "You heard him speak," I said. "Whatever I could say would be a lie."

"Not a lie and you know it. Smoke, I think you agree with Bill."

"That could be," I admitted. "Cord will raise hell when he finds out I've overstepped my authority."

"What can he do if you're right?" She put her hand on my arm. "What can he really do if we bring the farmers a little closer, make them understand that we're up against it as well as they are? Smoke, you believe in this, don't you?"

"Yeah," I said. Why fight it; this was what I asked myself. "All right, I'll go along with you."

She put her arms around me real quick and gave me a kiss that didn't last very long, but made me feel a little weak and lightheaded. For a long time I'd thought about this particular moment, and now that it had come and gone, I felt a little regret because it had taken me by surprise and I hadn't had a chance to really appreciate it.

We went out the front door and I walked to the barn for my horse while Julie brought her own around. Ma came out as we were about to leave, but she didn't say anything. The O'Dares rode in and out so blamed much that she had long ago given up trying to keep track of her family.

Since Vince Randolf was the big farmer on our side, I figured that we ought to visit him first, so we cut south toward his half-section. When Randolf first came to this country, he had a little money salted away and sank it all in his place, which made him a little better off and a little farther ahead than most of the others. First off, he bought a windmill and had a well driller come up from Guthrie and sink a well. This gave him all the drinking water he needed, plus enough to irrigate a three-acre garden patch, which, if the truth were known, was feeding the other three farmers on our side of the river. And Randolf was a better builder than the others. He'd bought sawed lumber for his house and in this way provided a little comfort for his wife and four children.

Vince Randolf wasn't much for fences either. He had a small one around his garden patch, but that was to keep his own milk cows from bloating themselves on greens. As we approached his place, Randolf came out, looking in our direction with a hand shielding his eyes. We drew up near his door and normally we would have dismounted, but with a farmer you're never sure of your welcome and we didn't want to give Randolf the idea that we were pushing ourselves onto anyone.

But he wasn't a man given to unfriendliness. He said, "Howdy. You look warm enough." We allowed that we were, then Randolf added, "Martha's got some cool buttermilk if you'd like some."

"That's sure kind of you," I said and jumped down so I could help Julie. Not that she really needed it, but it was something I liked to do and she let me enjoy myself.

Mrs. Randolf came to the door, a dry-faced woman with much of her youthful looks remaining. She wiped her hands on her apron, then went to the cistern while we followed Randolf into the house. The youngest played on the floor. He couldn't have been more than three and he promptly climbed up on my lap and made a grab for my hat. Randolf was all for making him get down but I gave him the hat to play with and he immediately pulled it down over his head so that only his chin was visible.

"Likely you've something on your mind," Randolf said. His wife came in with a tin of milk and set out the glasses. Buttermilk was something we never had at home; it's a farmer's drink and it sure cuts the thirst when the weather is hot.

"We've come," Julie said, "because we think it's time to talk out our problems."

"You speaking for Bill?"

Julie nodded.

Then Randolf looked at me. "I know how you O'Dares stick together so I won't even ask you."

"We think trouble's coming, Mr. Randolf," Julie said, "and we want to head it off."

"Good sentiment there," he admitted, "but trouble's been camping on my doorstep most of my life. Every time I hear that either of you find a calf missing, I expect to be rode on." He shook his head as though the whole affair saddened him beyond words. "It's not pleasant to live surrounded by unfriendly people. Live, knowing that any day one of them can ride up and forbid you to cross his property again." He looked directly at me. "And that's a legal right you O'Dares enjoy, son."

"Well now," I said hurriedly, "that's not likely to happen."

"You say that today. Tomorrow you may feel different." He sighed and folded his hands beneath the bib of his overalls. "Do you really believe Cord will ever give up enough land for a public road? You think he'd cut up his place just so's we'd have a legal right of way?" Randolf shook his head. "Cord's buying land, not giving it away." He paused to drink his buttermilk. "You go on down the line and talk to Wade Everett, or Higgins, or Mooney; they're all in the same fix. We all have the same fears."

"The O'Dares don't deal that way," I said, wishing there was some way to convince him, only there wasn't and we both knew it. A man didn't have to live in that part of the country long before he understood that Cord would do anything if he got his wind up.

"Let me tell you something," Randolf said. "We're no different from you, except that we farm and depend on what we grow for everything. I once farmed a piece of land that belonged to my grandfather. It was wore out when I came into it by inheritance. A man dreams of better things than he already has; if he don't he might as well be dead. So you see, we can understand, in a way, Cord's yearning for more, and we all know what it is to lose something you once had. But this is good land, son, and if it came to worse, I guess I'd kill to keep it. It's mine once I prove up on it, but I can't live knowing another man can legally keep me off it by forbidding me to trespass his property."

"Mr. Randolf," Julie said, "a court wouldn't allow anyone to do that to you."

"I guess I'd win my case all right," he admitted. "But justice is slow and it costs money. Money I don't have. But even if I had the money, my crops, my buildings would go to rack and ruin before I was allowed to come on my land." He looked at me. "Son, you came here to declare your good intentions, and I thank you for it, but the day hasn't arrived yet when a farmer dare trust a cattleman. The man on foot was never equal to the man on horse. No offense, but I'd appreciate it if you'd just leave us in peace."

What could a man say to an argument like that? He was right. As right as a man could be and just listening to him rattle off the truth like that made me feel pretty small. And what was worse, I couldn't do anything about it.

Julie and I finished our buttermilk, thanked Randolf and his wife for their hospitality and left. The young one cried when I took back my hat, but then you could say that he was just learning one of life's lessons earlier than usual.

8

Julie and I wore out the day going around from place to place. Alex Higgins was next, a bachelor who tried his best to make a go of the driest piece of land in Oklahoma. If he'd only had three hundred dollars for a well and windmill— but he didn't have, so why talk about it. I don't think he had three dollars. Higgins was polite enough, and embarrassed because he didn't have anything to offer us. And we were just as embarrassed trying to tell him that we didn't expect anything. Sure is strange what small things will do to a man's pride. We talked and he talked and we rode away knowing about as much as when we rode up. Higgins didn't hate a soul, according to him, but he made it plain that he was on the land and meant to stay, even if he starved to death, which seemed to be a likely prospect.

Dave Mooney was a tall man who moved slow and talked in jerks. His wife was heavy with child so we didn't stay long, since she seemed determined to cook us a meal. Mooney listened politely but you could see that he didn't believe a word of what we said. All the time I talked he kept eyeing me as though he suspected I'd whip out a gun and shoot both of them. Julie and I were both fairly discouraged by the time we cut east toward

Wade Everett's place on the way home.

I wasn't too sure what kind of a welcome awaited me at Everett's place; he'd been definite about how he felt the last time I was there. Yet I was counting on the man's fairness to remember who it was that pulled Luther off him. Everett was splitting kindling when we rode into the yard. He looked kind of surprised and a little worried. It was getting on toward mealtime, but he didn't invite us to dismount or eat.

From inside the shanty a baby wailed in a loud voice. Two other children poked their heads out, saw who it was and ducked back inside. It does something to a man when he sees people get that scared. Probably the mother used cattlemen for boogeymen when they wanted to make their young ones behave.

There wasn't much we could say to Everett, except what we had said to the others, and he listened with the same patience and that same flat refusal to believe in his eyes. By this time I was beginning to believe that Cord was right and I let Julie do all the talking. I kept watching the house, expecting to see a curl of cooking smoke spiral out of the chimney, or catch the flavors of supper, but there were neither of these things.

Under different circumstances I'd have never asked, but since Everett wasn't friendly to begin with, and I didn't care whether I hurt his feelings or not, I just came out with what was on my mind. "You folks got anything to eat? We're hungry."

Julie shot me an outraged glance, as though I'd lost my mind as well as my manners, but I ignored her. A sneaking suspicion was beginning to form in my mind and I wanted to test it out. I saw a brittle pride come into Wade Everett's lean face. He said, "We've already eaten."

"Smoke," Julie said quickly, "I think we'd better go." She was angry at my lapse of courtesy and the baby kept crying and Everett's claim to having already eaten just didn't ring true. With cattle or corn, you always work until the daylight is gone; a man ate when he couldn't do anything else.

"In a minute, Julie," I said and dismounted. Quickly I stepped to the soddy door and Wade Everett took a step toward me as though he intended to block me. Then all his pride ran out, leaving him round-shouldered and defeated in a way I never like to see a man defeated.

Now I've seen poor places in my life and have lived in a few myself, but the Everetts were living as close to the bottom as you can get without being dead. The beds for the kids were gunny sacks spread on the dirt floor. There was one table, completely bare, and three chairs made out of discarded packing crates. The baby was wailing when I stepped inside and Mrs. Everett put her hand over his mouth to still him.

There was a cupboard on the east wall, bare except for some salt and a pound or two of flour. I swung around, meaning to get out; I was mad as hell and wishing I wasn't. Everett's old trap-door Springfield was sitting by the door and I picked it up, snapped open the breech and found a live round there. Mrs. Everett, panic in her voice, shrilled, "What are you going to do? *Wade!*"

Everett, startled, started toward me, then stopped, unsure of what I meant by taking his gun. Stepping into the saddle, I spoke to Julie: "Wait here."

I cut along Wade Everett's fence until I came to the fringe of our herd. A young heifer strayed and when she saw me bearing down, turned and began to run. I dismounted quickly, sighted the .45-70 and touched her off. Recoil cracked me back a step and the heifer bawled once, did a flip and lay a moment with her legs kicking.

The roar of the gun and the smell of blood nearly spooked my pony for I had to fight him a moment before I could mount. Then I had him under control and the rest was easy. I put a rope around the dead heifer and dragged her to Wade Everett's front yard. He just stood there and stared at me when I handed him back his rifle.

"You can skin her out and have some hot broth in that kid's belly by nine o'clock," I told him. "Let's go, Julie."

Everett's mouth was working, trying to thank me, I guess, but nothing came out. Besides, we were riding out at a smart pace and I would have kept it up if Julie hadn't reached over, grabbed the bridle and pulled my pony down to a walk.

I was feeling a little ashamed for letting another man's poverty get to me; Cord always said that a man had to be tough to last. Julie understood this, I guess. I sure didn't have to tell her what Cord would say about it. But the fact that she understood why I did it made everything all right. I didn't give a damn just then whether Cord liked this or not.

"You did a nice thing, Smoke. Very nice."

"Cord won't think so," I said. "But when I saw that kid, half starved, I got mad, Julie. Mad at all the things that we have to put up with every day."

"I guess you had better not tell Cord," she said. "We'll keep this between ourselves, Smoke. You and me."

Suddenly things seemed a little brighter; I grinned at her. "All right, Julie. To hell with Cord."

"Race you to the river?"

"You got a race," I said and kicked my pony into a run.

She beat me, strictly honest. We dismounted and sat on the bank and watched the night sweep over the land. When it was time to go, Julie said, "Come over with me, Smoke."

"Well, I ought to get home. Ma and Edna are alone. No telling when Cord or Luther will show up."

"I'll make muffins," she offered.

That did the trick. "You've got an extra mouth to feed," I said and we swung up, splashing across the river a moment later. We rode at an easy walk the rest of the way and when we ame into the yard, we found Bill Hageman sitting on the porch. Julie turned the horses over to Charlie Davis, one of the two hands who worked for them, then joined us on the porch.

Bill took the cigarette from his mouth and said, "Any luck?"

"They listened," Julie said, "but that was all."

Bill grunted. "I gave Cord credit for being more persuasive than that."

"He didn't go," I said. "I did." There was a brief silence while Bill figured this one out.

"Cord know about it?"

"No," I said.

Another silence, then Bill said, "Cord likes to run things himself, the O'Dare business and anything else that comes his way. But you did the right thing, Smoke. Believe that."

"I believe it or I wouldn't have gone along."

That was the truth, but I still had a growing concern about what Cord would do when he found out. I had broken one of his cardinal rules by acting on my own, a thing we O'Dares never did.

Bill Hageman ground out his cigarette with his boot and stood up. "I think I'll go into town, Julie. Cord may be there and I might get a chance to talk to him." He looked at me and grinned. "I won't say anything about your visiting, Smoke."

"I appreciate that."

He started off the porch, then stopped. "I'm moving my herd tomorrow, Smoke. Are your cars waiting on the siding?"

"Cord said he'd taken care of it."

Bill Hageman grunted softly. "Then they'll be there. Cord always does what he says. That's why I worry when he talks about hanging." He walked across the yard to get his horse and I followed Julie into the house.

She also kept her word and made up a pan of muffins for the oven. I sat at the kitchen table and watched her as she moved about. She warmed up some cold meat and fried a skillet full of potatoes. I never tired of looking at her for she was slim-waisted, quick-moving, with a grace that reminded me of a young elk.

And she knew that I watched her; I think she welcomed it. Once she turned her head and said,

"How many meals do you suppose I've cooked for you?"

"A couple dozen?"

"More like a hundred," she said. "You ate my first pie, even though it was terrible."

"As I recall, it was good," I said. "But the ones you bake now are some better though."

"Everything gets better with repetition, Smoke."

The muffins were finally ready to take out of the oven and we ate our late supper with nothing separating us except the lamplight and a silence that I liked. Not a stiff silence where two people just have nothing to talk about; rather it was a silence fostered by two who had never needed a lot of talk.

I helped Julie with the dishes, then we went out to sit on the front porch and test the cool night breeze. Charlie and the other hand were cleaning out the bunkhouse, getting ready to leave for good in the morning because a man with scarcely thirty head of cattle didn't need paid hands.

Julie watched them for a while. "We're back where we started, Bill and I."

"You going to hang onto the place?"

"We have to," she said. "It takes money to move, and Bill's spent it all here, on this house, the barn, and the well on the south section." She shook her head sadly. "I don't mind starting over from nothing, but not being able to get ahead wears on a person."

"That's what Cord says. Only he blames the farmers. Says we ought to have more land."

"Land," she said softly. "Men lie for it, kill for it, and then it doesn't rain for a year and it all blows away. That doesn't make sense, Smoke."

"Sure could stand some rain all right," I said. She looked at me and I pretended to study something out in the dark yard. Being around her like this was what I wanted more than anything else, but I ran out of talk. Not that I didn't have anything to say. When I was alone I could think of a million things to say, and all of them leading to something romantic. "Thought I saw clouds this morning," I said. "Guess not though. Nothin' ever came of it."

Julie kept on looking at me and I began to wish she'd stop. "Smoke, what are you thinking about?"

Cord would have told her, but I couldn't be bold like that. I could only come up with a half-truth. "I guess I think about you most of the time, Julie."

"That's hardly fair to you, Smoke. I don't think of you all the time."

"I know that," I said. "I guess I ain't much, compared to Cord."

She turned sideways in her rocker. "Smoke,

don't ever compare yourself with Cord. You love me, don't you?"

"Yes," I admitted, "but I've never mentioned it before."

"You didn't have to," Julie said. "I knew, Smoke, but I didn't want to let on that I knew. I never wanted a weapon that was capable of hurting you."

"What weapon?" I didn't know what she was talking about.

"When you love me, you give me the power to hurt you. I never wanted that power, but you forced it on me."

"That's all right," I told her. "I'll take the chance."

"It's not all right!" Her sharpness came as a surprise, then she made her voice soft again. "I wish I could say that I love you, Smoke, but I don't think you'd want me to say it if I wasn't sure."

"I guess it's Cord you love," I said. "It sort of figures."

"Love him? I don't think so. Yet there's an excitement about him that I've never found in another man. Unfortunately most women have found it too, so my discovery is not exactly original. He's like a wild horse, Smoke. Very handsome and very dangerous and there's always that challenge there, asking you to try and tame him. You may know that others have tried and failed, but pride, being what it is, convinces you that you might be the one to succeed." She looked at me, then reached out for my hand. "Smoke, I don't love him. I'm just—fascinated by him."

"I guess that settles that," I said. "I sure ain't very fascinatin'."

"You aren't your own man either," she said bluntly. "If you want to know the truth, no woman could take you seriously because if you said some-thing today, there's no guarantee that tomorrow Cord wouldn't send you around to take it back."

"That sure as hell paints me a prime jackass," I said. If I sounded bitter it was because I was. No man likes to be reminded that he's second best all the time, not even to his own brother.

When I got up and stepped past her, she said, "Looks like I've said too much."

"It's been aplenty."

Her hand came out and held me. "Smoke, I'm sorry. But you wanted the truth, didn't you?"

The truth or a lie? What was the difference? The impulse hit me and I reached for her, not easy like I'd always figured on doing, but rough, a man's way when he is determined to take what he wants and all her hollering be damned. She came to her feet and against me hard enough to jar some of the breath from her. Then I had her locked tight in my arms and was kissing her, not gently, but with enough stored-up passion to let her know size wasn't a handicap.

When I turned her loose, she stood there looking a little bewildered. I had the wind up then and really spouted off. "Is that what you want? A lot of bruises that you can admire in front of your mirror after a buggy ride? Hell, you don't have to go to Cord if that's what you're after." I grabbed my hat and stomped off the porch, pausing in the yard. "And you want to know something else? You got nothing a man'd fight over. I've seen reservation squaws that kiss a lot better."

This last was a bald-faced lie if I ever told one, but I was mad, along with being confused and wishing I had a double-jointed leg so I could clout myself. A man turns into a blamed fool after he's made a mistake in front of a woman; *I* did anyway.

Julie called after me but I didn't stop. I just fetched my horse and got on him, striking out for the river. Every step he took was counted and regretted because I really wanted to go back and tell her how sorry I was. But I wasn't a big enough man to do that and this was something she could rightly hold against me.

9

There was no pausing at the river for me; the wind through the cottonwoods was way off key, a moan instead of a song. I wasn't so sure the pleasant sounds would ever come back either. Even the home place seemed deserted, so dark and silent. After putting up my horse I walked slowly toward the house. I tried to be quiet but Ma heard me and called from her room. "Is that you, Smoke?"

"Yeah, Ma. Cord and Luther home?"

"Not yet, son." I heard the bed rustle as she resettled herself and then I went into the kitchen to light the lamp and make a pot of coffee. While the water heated, I heard a door open and a moment later Edna came in, blinking against the light. She wore a blue satin robe, tight drawn to reveal her finely curved shape.

"Have you seen Luther, Smoke?"

"No. Want some coffee?"

She shook her head. "It'll keep me awake." She sat down at the table and rubbed her eyes with the heel of her hand. "You don't know where he went?"

"Maybe over to Rindo's Springs," I said. "He's friendly with Heck Overland."

"I don't like being left alone," Edna said. "Luther knows that." She glanced at my cup of coffee, then added, "I believe I'll have some of that after all. It smells fine."

I poured a cup for her, then shoved the canned milk and sugar her way; she stirred with a slow, listless motion, then drank, looking at me over the rim of the cup.

"Something bothering you, Edna?"

She seemed surprised. "Do I look like something's bothering me?"

"Sort of," I said. "You and Luther have a spat?"

"No," she said quickly. "It's nothing, Smoke. Nothing at all."

"If you ever want to tell me anything, you'll find that I listen real good."

Her smile was quick and genuine. "I'm sure you do, but there are some things talk will not cure." She sat there, sipping her coffee and watching me. "Maybe I should tell you. I thought we were going to have a place of our own, Luther and me. But every time I mention it he gets mad."

"I thought you liked it here?"

"Sure I like it but people have to do for themselves, Smoke. Luther has to get away from here. From Cord and Ma. I'm not saying anything against either of them, but Luther needs to be his own boss."

"Well," I said, "if Luther wants to go all he has to do is to saddle his horse."

"Are you sure that's all, Smoke?"

"What do you mean, is that all? Sure, that's all. You think Cord would try and stop him?"

"I think that Cord would . . ." She suddenly closed her mouth and took her cup to the sink. "It doesn't matter what I think. Good night."

I watched her leave and after I heard her door close, I sat there and tried to figure out what she was getting at. I was still trying to figure it as I undressed for bed, but I could attach no sensible meaning to it.

Besides, Julie kept popping into my thoughts, along with all the foolish things I had said and for a time I writhed in self-loathing. There wasn't much use thinking about the Grange dance; I'd shot that where it hurts with my big mouth and grabbing hands. Cord wouldn't have to work very hard now to collect his dollar bet; I'd made things pretty easy for him.

The next morning I got up before Ma or Edna, fixed a hasty breakfast and was riding toward Wade Everett's place before the grayness of dawn started to thin out the darker shades of night. Cord and Luther were still absent; I'd checked the barn and their horses were gone. This put me in a sour frame of mind for the work fell on my shoulders, too much work. There was some doubt whether I'd even get the herd to town alone; a man can't ride drag and flankers at the same time.

Then I recalled the small favor I'd done Wade Everett and headed directly for his place. He was up; there was a lamp shining through the open doorway. He heard me approaching and stuck his head out the door. I made sure that I dismounted in the light and when he saw who it was, he beckoned me inside.

They were eating beefsteak for breakfast. The little one was sucking on a piece of fat and he looked as though he hadn't cried for days.

"I wish I had some coffee to offer," Wade Everett said.

I waved it aside. "Had breakfast, thanks. But I could use a favor."

"Well, I'm certainly owing you one. Name it."

I explained about Luther and Cord being gone and how I could use some help with the cattle. Everett allowed that he wasn't much of a horseman and much less a cowboy, but he'd be glad to oblige. He sat down to finish off his breakfast but before he did, the rumble of a wagon came across the flats, then drove into the yard.

Everett and I looked out just as Julie Hageman was dismounting. She saw me and said, "Help me unload this, Smoke."

"What's this?" Everett asked, but Julie didn't bother about answering him. She hefted thirty pounds of Arbuckle's coffee and carried it into the house. Seems like she brought everything the cook shack held: four hundred pounds of potatoes, rice, kidney beans, Mexican browns, sugar, flour, a side of bacon and some salt pork. Mrs. Everett was happy, so she cried, and Wade was too choked up to speak.

Julie explained it. "We paid off the crew and this was left. Didn't want it to go to waste."

Sure was a thin lie, that. Everett recognized it, but it spared his pride, and that was important. With the food stowed, Julie got back on the wagon. I wanted to talk to her, explain if I could, how the devil could get into a man and goad him into all sorts of fool things, but the explanation stuck in my throat.

"Are you driving to the railhead this morning, Smoke?"

"With Everett's help," I said.

"Why don't you meet us at the river? Charlie and Russ will help you."

"Thanks," I said. She lifted the reins to move out. "Julie, about last night . . ."

"Some other time, Smoke."

I stood there as she wheeled out of Everett's yard; she was mad at me all right and I really didn't blame her.

Wade Everett didn't own a saddle horse, just an old mare who had spent her years behind a plow or wagon. Yet I was surprised at the way she caught onto tricks from my pony. Pretty clumsy on her feet, I discovered, but she had a level head and worked the drag without a hitch.

By eight o'clock we had them pushing along the wash, Everett on drag and me racing around the flanks. Between a nimble pony and a snapping lariat I managed to keep them pointed toward the river. The dust was wicked and Everett was having a rough time out there on the tail end, but the herd moved right along and I knew that he was doing a good job.

Had Luther or Cord been along I'd have cut directly toward the road, but without that extra flanker, I had to move toward the cottonwood-lined river, figuring the critters wouldn't bolt through the trees. The guess was pretty good and we made fair time. Nine o'clock found us north of the home place and then I spotted Bill Hageman's herd on the other side of the river.

Julie was there with her wagon and Charlie Davis waved his slicker, telling me to drive across. Everett thought I was crazy when I turned the cattle into the water, but he kept them coming and I joined him at the drag to haze the last over to the other shore.

With the two herds combined, talk was impossible. Charlie Davis was a little surprised to see a farmer chasing cattle on a plow horse, but he didn't laugh and I silently thanked him for that. I joined Wade Everett and the two of us ate dust all the way to Ponca City.

Mixing our herds like this would make a mess of it at the loading chute. We'd have to tally as they went into the cars, but the extra trouble was already outweighed by the ease in which we drove, now that we had a man on each flank and two on drag.

Through the morning I kept looking for Cord or Luther to show up, but neither of them did. We skirted Ponca City and came in east of the depot, holding the herd near the loading pens. The cattle buyer was there, a small, round-bellied man in a derby hat. He edged close in his buggy and said, "Whose brand is this?"

"We're mixed," I said. Charlie Davis came up, flailing dust from his clothes. Sweat made muddy streaks down his lean face.

The buyer wasn't too happy with the herd jumbled, but this was our problem, not his. "How many you got?" he asked of Charlie Davis.

"Close to two hundred," he said, then looked at me. "How about you, Smoke?"

"About a hundred and ten," I said. "Give or take a couple."

The buyer pursed his lips. "I'll accept your tally. Count 'em as they go into the cars. You can drive 'em."

He wheeled his buggy around and stormed away. Bill Hageman was coming toward us from the main part of town. He pulled up and said, "Charlie, you push 'em toward the chute. Smoke and I'll tally."

"Sure thing," Davis said and rode back to

where Wade Everett and Charlie's partner waited.

"How did you get Everett in on this?" Bill asked.

"I asked him."

"You're a persuasive cuss," Bill admitted.

We tied our horses near the chute and got out our pocket knives and a piece of wood to whittle. That may sound a little odd, but it's a carry-down from the days when few men knew their numbers; the notches on a stick are as permanent as writing on paper. We perched on the fence and counted out the brands.

Loading is always a filthy job. The dust and noise close out everything else. Cars were filled and then the little Simcoe switcher would hiss and bang another in place, adding to the string from the dead car siding. There was no knocking off for dinner; we stayed at it until mid-afternoon and then the last car was filled. Bill and I both signed the buyer's books while he went to the bank for the money.

Wade Everett came over, a very tired man. "If you'll not be needing me any longer, I think I'll be getting home." He patted the mare's neck. "Harriet's had a tryin' day."

"I'm certainly obliged to you," I said.

"I'm the one who's obliged," Everett said and rode away, elbows and legs flapping.

Bill Hageman stared after him, then said, "What do you suppose he meant by that?"

"I'll have to ask him the next time I see him."

We walked together to Lanahan's Saloon. Charlie Davis and his partner joined us at the bar and I was a little embarrassed because I didn't have a nickel in my pocket with which to stand treat, and I owed the treat. But I didn't let a lack of money stop me. Business was thin and Lanahan looked at each of us.

"I'm buying," I said.

"Well," Lanahan said, "I've got slow poison or quick."

"Slow for me," Charlie Davis said. "You, Russ?"

"Beer," Russ said.

"Four beers then," I said, and after Lanahan drew them, added, "Just put that on the account, Pete."

He looked at me odd and quick. "We don't charge drinks around here, Smoke."

"You do today," I said, giving him a blunt, affronted stare. "Hell, you'll get your twenty cents!"

Pete Lanahan grinned foolishly. "Yeah. What am I saying?"

Charlie Davis wasn't a man for talk; neither was his partner, which was probably why they got on so well together. Bill nursed his beer for| a while, then I called for a refill all around. Finally the cattle buyer came in, a cold cigar clamped between his teeth. He had a fist full of bills and began to count it out, shoving a pile toward Bill Hageman, and the other to me. I paid Pete Lanahan his forty cents and pocketed the rest. Charlie Davis drained what remained of his beer and said, "We'd best be riding, Bill."

Solemnly, Bill Hageman counted out their wages. "I wish I could keep you both," he said, "but I just can't."

"We understand," Davis said. "Maybe we'll see you again."

"I hope so," Bill said, but I felt sure that neither would ever come back. The West was full of men like Davis and his partner, nice enough men, but drifters with no home place of their own. A man had to have a home place somewhere, a place where he belonged and could always call his own. I couldn't help but feel sorry for both of them, but they wouldn't have understood my feelings if I had spoken of them.

After they went out the cattle buyer ordered whiskey. When he drank, he flipped his head back, held the whiskey in his mouth for a minute, then swallowed it. Bill Hageman said, "I'll see you, Smoke."

"Thanks for the help."

He grinned and waved and went outside to mount his horse. After he rode down the street, the cattle buyer said, "There goes a man who's finished."

"Bill?"

"Yep. He thinks he can ride this out, but in two

years he'll find out that he can't get to his feet." He spoke without looking at me. "The range is drying up. Another year of this and there won't be enough for the grasshoppers to come after."

"We'll get rain," I said. "It's been dry before but there's always rain."

He laughed and shook his head. "I see a lot of country; I know what I'm saying." He looked at me. "You people never give up, do you?" He ordered another whiskey but did not drink it immediately. "Kid, in this country you have to have land. A lot of land to carry you through the dry years. Sixty acres at least for every head you run. The good years, when there's plenty of water and grass, you can cut that to a steer for every fifteen, but you've got to have land to take care of the dry spells." He slapped me on the back. "You O'Dares used to have that kind of land before the government moved you out. You listen to Cord, kid. He knows he's got to have land. A hell of a lot more than he has now."

The buyer paid for his drinks and went out. I stood there with Lanahan and listened to the botflies drone around the beer taps. Finally I asked, "Them flies ever get drunk on that?"

"Never watched 'em to find out," Lanahan said. "You want another beer? On the house."

"In that case, yes," I said.

When Lanahan straightened with a foamy stein, he said, "That fella made sense, Smoke.

Bill don't know it, but he's through, selling off that way. He'll stick it out for a year or two, but he'll never survive it." He paused to strip a wrapper from a cigar. "How many head you got left now?"

"Maybe a hundred and fifty—two hundred."

Lanahan shook his head. "That Cord. Don't see how he does it, but he hangs on. Determined, that's what I call him. Watches his nickels and hangs on while the others drop off. You think he'll try and buy up Hageman's place?"

"Bill wouldn't sell."

"Maybe he won't have any choice," Lanahan said. He tapped his finger on the bar. "Wouldn't surprise me a bit if Cord ain't put aside a few nickels just for that purpose. Cord's a planner, Smoke. You got to give him credit for that. He don't do nothing without having it figured beforehand which way it's going to come out."

10

Pete Lanahan was sure a windy cuss when he got wound up and since I didn't have anything better to do, I stood there and listened. I nursed the free beer until it got warm, then offended Lanahan by not buying another one.

A horseman came into town at a gallop and Lanahan and I turned our heads toward the door as Luther dismounted out front. "Hot to be running a horse," Lanahan said.

Luther stumbled when he came onto the saloon porch. His face was flushed and from the irregularity of his step I knew that he'd had a few too many at Heck Overland's place in Rindo's Springs. He saw me standing there and came up, flinging an arm around me, whether in brotherly love or searching for support, I didn't know.

"The bottle," he said to Lanahan, then stared at him until it was placed on the bar, along with a clean glass. Luther poured a shot that was too big and then drank it as though it were pink lemonade. He stood there, blinking away the tears and breathing through his open mouth.

"Ain't you had enough?" I asked.

He looked at me in that studied way all drunks have. "I've just started, boy."

When he reached again for the bottle, I just pushed it out of his way. Lanahan picked it up and set it beneath the bar. Luther looked at me, then at Lanahan. "Aaaaay! What is thish?"

"Let's go home," I suggested, taking him by the arm.

"That's a quarter for the drink," Lanahan said. "He had a double."

I pulled out the roll and the change and gave him a quarter. While I was digging it out, Luther reached over and snatched the bills from my hand. There was nearly three thousand dollars in that wad, enough to feed a family for nearly three years at the going rate. I tried to grab it back but he was retreating.

"Ooooo!" he said. "Look at all that money."

"You'd better give me that," I said, trying not to excite him. It was like watching a baby pick up a sharp knife by the blade. Instinct says to grab it away from him but reason tells you you'll cut off his fingers if you do. I groped for something to distract Luther. "Come on and have another drink, Luther."

He grinned. "Naaaaa! This is better than whiskey. I just want to hold it. Never had that much money before." He fanned the ends of the bills. "Sure a lot of money, Smoke. Won't have to ask ol' Cord for money now, will I?"

"Come on, Luther. Give me the money and let's go home."

"I'm not ready to go yet," he said. Before I could stop him he lurched out of the place, driving off the porch and across the street.

Pete Lanahan said, "You'd better get that damned fool, Smoke."

Pete didn't often come up with words of wisdom, but that sure made sense. With Luther drunk, there was no telling what he would do next, and whichever way it went, Cord was going to blame me.

By the time I got to Lanahan's door, Luther was staggering into the mercantile. A couple of blanketed Indians were dozing in the shade; they scattered before Luther's howling approach. I ducked under the hitch rail and ran after him, only he was inside and running everyone else out before I could get to him. A pair of Ponca City's spinsters were at the dry goods counter and before they could yell—and I wondered later if they wanted to—Luther had grabbed them, kissed them, and turned them free. They put on a good show of indignation but I'll lay money that was all they talked about for months.

Luther had the dry goods section to himself now and was pawing over the dresses. Felix Huddlemeyer, who owned the place, just stood with his mouth open, wondering whether he dared cross Luther or not. When he saw me, and that I was sober, his expression changed to one of hope.

Now Huddlemeyer's stock had never been

what you could call fancy, and because he was the town's biggest tightwad, his inventory was pretty low. Luther had gathered up everything on the counter and was staggering toward Huddlemeyer. "Take 'em all," Luther was saying. "Buy every damn one. Show him that a man can give his wife a pretty or two if he wants."

About then I got a grip on Luther's arm and instead of pulling him around, only succeeded in breaking him free of the dresses. They fell to the floor and were promptly trampled. Luther stepped around like a man dancing for the first time, only he hooked his spurs into the goods, ripping several dresses. Huddlemeyer clapped both hands to his head and closed his eyes.

"Let's get out of here, Luther. I mean it!"

He tried to swing on me, the money still clutched in his fist. Ducking was easy and then I belted him solidly on the jaw. He went limp and I bent over, letting him drape over my shoulder.

The money fluttered down like green leaves and Huddlemeyer looked at it.

"Would you pick that up for me?" I asked.

He hurried around the counter and picked up every bill; Huddlemeyer had a native tenderness toward money. "My goods," he wailed. "It's ruined."

"When he's sober he'll come back and settle up," I said. I took the money, stuffed it in my back pocket and walked out.

Things like that always draw a crowd and the

crowd drew a lot of conclusions, most of which I knew I wouldn't like. Trying to explain something like this was useless so I just pressed through and laid Luther facedown across his horse. I mounted and led the way out of town, keeping to a slow walk so he wouldn't fall off.

He didn't stay out very long, but the combination rap on the jaw and riding head down made him powerful sick. Luther slid to the ground and spent ten or fifteen mighty rough minutes. When he straightened up his face was ashen and he had a bad case of the shakes.

"You made a damn fool of yourself," I told him.

He looked at me as though he had never seen me before. "Who the hell cares?"

"I care," I told him. "Now get on your horse and let's get home."

"You giving me orders, Smoke?"

"You take it any way you want. When you prove, like you just did, that you can't handle yourself, then somebody has to do it for you."

He glared at me, as if everything was my fault, then the anger ran out of him, leaving him sad and whipped and hating himself. "I wanted to show Edna that I could do for myself," he said. "You can understand that, can't you, Smoke?"

"I guess so."

He took off his hat and wiped his arm across his forehead. "I've been thinking about her all night, and the drunker I got, the farther away became the answers. A man's got to break away, Smoke. He's got to or he'll never amount to a damned thing."

"Then take Edna and leave," I said. "I'd do it."

"Would you? You've got three thousand there. Take it and ride out now. Go somewhere and live your own life."

"The money's not mine," I said. "It belongs to all of us."

"We'll never see any of it," he said. He looked like a man who was about to cry and I didn't like to see him that way; he was almost a total stranger. "A man never sees anything until it's too late, Smoke. Kind of had a nagging feeling from the beginning, that Cord was setting something up between me and Edna. But I wasn't thinking of her, Smoke. Not for a minute. Just thought of myself and what being married would mean. I figured that being married would change every-thing, make me my own man. But it sure didn't. Cord, he knew it wouldn't all the time and let me go through with it so he could laugh at me." Luther's face screwed up ugly and wild-eyed and he hit himself in the chest with his fist. "He even picked out my woman for me! You know that? Picked her out and paid her train fare and the preacher!"

"You're talking wild," I said. "Hell, Cord don't mean anything to be like that."

Luther looked at me wonderingly, like I was

some innocent babe wandering into a danger I was too green to understand. "You can't see him yet, can you, Smoke? You can't see him at all." He shook his head as though it was too bad. "He's laughing, Smoke. Not out loud, but he's laughing just the same. I'm trapped and there's no way out of the cage. You'll be trapped too. Oh, yes you will. One of these days you'll want to step out and then he'll trap you too."

"You're still drunk," I said.

He didn't answer me. He just climbed on his horse, whirled and struck out toward the home place as fast as he could ride. I looked after him for a moment, toying with the idea of letting him ride it out of his system, but decided that the risks were too great; he might fall and break his fool neck. So I gigged my pony into motion. There was no catching him; he rode like demons were after him, but I didn't lose too much ground, arriving at home about ten minutes after Luther did.

From the barn I could hear Ma crying and Edna scolding, and overriding this was Luther's angry voice. I hurried to the house. They were standing in the hall and Luther had a blanket roll over his shoulder. Ma was standing there with tears running down her cheeks and kneading her hands together. Edna had a good grip on Luther's shirt front and was trying to hold him, but he was dragging her toward the front door.

When he saw me standing there, he said, "Don't try and stop me, Smoke."

"This time you can do as you danged please," I told him.

Ma turned to me, wailing, "He's leaving! Make him stay!"

"Let go of me!" Luther said, trying to free himself from Edna's grip.

"Luther, please wait! What did I do? I've got a right to know what I've done?"

"You ain't done a damned thing," Luther said. "Are you going to let go or do I have to belt you one?"

The way he said it, calm and kind of wicked, shocked her and she turned him loose. From the way he'd been struggling to get out the door you'd think he'd cut and run, but he didn't. He just stood there, looking at Ma and Edna.

I said, "Thought you were so all-fired anxious to leave?"

"I'm going," he said. "Good-bye, Ma, Edna."

"Where?" Ma asked. "Luther, where? What for?"

"I don't know where," he said. "Ma, I just don't know!"

"You'll send for me, won't you, Luther?" asked Edna.

He didn't answer her. Ma covered her face with her apron and cried in a loud, distressed voice. "Oh, if Cord were only here you wouldn't do this!"

"It must be my fault," Edna said. "But how, Luther? I love you. I came out here and married you. There has to be a reason!"

"Ask Cord," Luther said. "He's got an answer for everything." He turned away then and as I stood in the doorway blocking the exit, he stopped. "Do I have to move you out of the way, Smoke?"

"I don't think you could, but I'm going to move anyway."

Luther went out, plunging off the porch as though he had to hurry before he changed his mind. Ma took her wailing to the kitchen and Edna watched, slack-faced, not able to make sense of this. She wanted to cry, but I give her credit, she held the tears back.

Since Luther's horse was pretty well run out, he saddled a fresh one. I watched him from the door, as did Edna. She said, "Do you know why, Smoke?"

"He'll come back," I said, all of a sudden very positive about this. "He'll be back, Edna. It's a failing of his."

I turned to go into the kitchen to be with Ma but Edna grabbed me and pulled me around to face her. "What do you mean, failing? How can coming back be a failing? He belongs here."

I shook my head. "The trouble with Luther is that he don't belong anywhere. My trouble too."

This only added to Edna's confusion but she

let go of my arm and I went into the kitchen. Ma didn't look up when I sat down across from her at the table. She kept her eyes closed and tears squeezed out. "If Cord were only here," she kept saying. "He'd know what to do. Cord can hold us together, just like your father used to; he's so much like him."

"Luther'll be back, Ma." I put my hand over hers. "He won't go far. He'll come back in a day or so."

She raised her hands to brush away the tears, then smiled. "Of course, I ought to know better. He's mad about something now, but he'll get over it and come back. Luther loves us. He'd never leave us."

She was right; I had to admit it. But she was wrong about the reasons. Luther would come back all right, but not because he loved us so much. He'd come back because he was afraid. I couldn't tell Ma that; she'd never believe me. So I said, "You just keep thinking that, Ma."

I couldn't bear to sit there any longer so I went outside and perched on the back steps. Being alone with my thoughts didn't help much, but I no longer had to keep my guard up so Ma wouldn't guess how deeply I was troubled. Ma's remark about Cord being like Pa stuck in my mind and wouldn't go away. And the more I thought about it, the more resemblance I saw. Not physical, but in character and temperament.

I was having diffi-culty deciding whether this was good or bad. Bad for Luther anyway. He was a sensitive man to begin with and twenty-some years under the thumb gave him a serious doubt as to his own ability to act by himself.

Then I wondered why I wasn't like that? Probably too ornery. Sneaky, Cord sometimes called it, because he'd tell me to do a thing, and if I felt like it, I'd do it, and if I didn't, I'd take the licking or wait until his back was turned, then do as I danged pleased. Luther could never do that. Wasn't put together like that, I guess, and Cord knew it. Of course, having a head full of foolishness, I never noticed all this while it was going on, but now that I thought about it, I could see a thousand small ways in which Luther had been bent until he grew to be nothing.

There was no telling how far Luther'd get before he decided to come back, but I was dead sure that he would turn around. In a way he had told me as much there at the edge of town. A man can be torn in two and you can live with him and never know it until it's too late to do anything about it. Looking back now, I wish I'd let him buy the dresses for Edna. Then he'd have had to face Cord and take his licking. That way, Luther would have at least tried. But like a fool, I took that away from him too.

11

Ma and Edna ate supper alone; I didn't bother to go in. I walked out past the barn and watched the sunset, conscious of the three thousand dollars in my pocket and toying with the thought of saddling my pony and lighting out for California or Wyoming. But that kind of card dealing isn't in me, so I ended up cussing myself for having the idea in the first place.

Edna came out and stood on the edge of the porch. She saw me and called, "Will you hitch up the buggy, Smoke? Ma's tired of staying home so I thought we'd go into town to the dance."

I pulled the buggy out of the lean-to, then got out the harness horses. They hadn't been exercised for a few days and were full of Old Nick, but I shouldered them between the traces and hooked up. Ma had on her velvet dress and beads and the ridiculous hat. As always, I helped her into the buggy and Edna took the reins when I handed them to her.

"I wish you wouldn't mope around here, Smoke," Ma said.

"Luther may come back," I said. "You go on, Ma. Have a good time."

She bent and patted my cheek. "You're such a good boy, Smoke."

I stood there while they drove from the yard, then went over to the porch and sat down. Luther, hell! The only reason I didn't have my suit on now was that I didn't want to face Julie Hageman after shooting off my mouth.

Night came in quiet and fast, and with it, a feeling of loneliness I'd never known before. The wind began to pick up, scuffing dust along, banging a loose stall door in the barn. Time passes slow when a man is alone; I sat for hours and they seemed like days. Once I went inside to look at the kitchen clock; a quarter after ten, then once more I took my place on the porch.

A faint sound coming from the direction of the river pulled my attention up sharp and I sat perfectly still, listening. Then I heard it again, a horse. No, two horses, and the creak of a buggy. Finally, I saw the rig moving toward the yard, and I stepped away from the house.

I recognized Julie Hageman before she saw me, and when she did, she seemed startled because she suddenly sawed on the reins. I held the nervous horses for a moment, then stepped to the off wheel. I could see that she had on a light-colored dress, the kind with a lot of ruffles, and from beneath the hem lace petticoats peeked out.

She said, "I waited, Smoke, but you didn't come."

"I didn't think I'd be welcome," I told her.

"We both said things we shouldn't have," Julie said. "Smoke, I just can't stay mad at you!"

"You seemed mad at Everett's place."

"I was pretending, but I can't do that well either." She looked at me and waited. "Well, are you going to take me to the dance or not?"

"Give me ten minutes," I said and ran toward the house.

Some people would say that a man can't take a cold water bath, change his clothes and slick his hair in ten minutes, but I'll tell you that I did it in eight, even. And I shaved too and didn't nick myself once.

Julie gave the reins to me once I'd hopped aboard and I whipped the light buggy around and drove from the yard. I didn't say anything for a while, not that I didn't have anything on my mind, but I was trying not to put my foot in my mouth again. Yet a man can't drive all the way to town without saying something.

"Sure glad shipping's over."

"I'm glad I got up the nerve to come across the river," she said.

"Huh?" I stared at her.

"Smoke, can you forget the schoolgirl things I said?"

"Didn't sound schoolgirlish to me," I said.

She reached across and took the reins, pulling the span to a halt. "Smoke, you kissed me the

146

other night, but not the way you wanted to. You kissed me like you thought I wanted to be kissed." She wrapped the reins around the whip socket and took my hands and placed them on her waist. "Now, I want you to kiss me like you want to."

Whatever folks have said about me, one thing they all know is that I don't need a lot of urging. I'll never forget how soft she felt in my arms, or how the heat of her pushed right through my serge suit, or how her lips answered me in a way I'd always wanted them to answer. My experience with women was limited, sure enough, but I could tell that I'd made an impression. Her eyes had a bright shine in their depths and her smile was for me alone.

"Smoke," she said, "are there really reservation squaws who . . ."

The best way to make women shut up, I had just discovered, was to kiss them, which I did. Her arms knocked my hat off and liked to choke me, but can you name a better way to die? When I released her, I said, "Don't you worry about any other woman, Julie."

I unwrapped the reins and drove on. She put her arm through mine and laid her head against my shoulder. And that's the way we drove to Ponca City, only it took a little longer than usual because I had to stop three or four times to see if that kiss had lost anything.

It hadn't.

The Grange Hall was on the west side of town, between the school and the church. It had been built like a barn and now it was bright with light and music floated toward us as we tied up in the lot behind. Buggies and saddle horses were thick beneath the cottonwood grove and I had a time finding a place to tie up. Finally I wedged in between a farmer's wagon and Doc Lamson's sulky. I helped Julie down and we started for the hall.

"Wait! I forgot my box lunch." She hurried back to the rig to get it.

"What kind of a ribbon do you have on it?" I asked.

"Blue. Are you going to bid on it, Smoke?"

"You're darned tootin' I am! You think I want some other fella dancing with my girl all night."

Something I said there had the kind of effect I liked; she stepped close to me and pressed her lips against mine. Then she took my hand and we went on in.

The dance had been under way for nearly two hours. Ma and Edna were there and Edna was dancing with Bill Hageman. Julie spoke briefly to Ma, then took her box lunch to the auctioneer's table at the end of the hall. I followed her, moving easy through the crowd. People spoke to me, farmers and townsfolk. I saw Vince Randolf and two other farmers by the refreshment table.

When I nodded to Randolf, he waved and smiled.

Julie and I swung onto the floor and for the next half-hour time sort of got lost for me. When the set was finished, I got her a glass of punch, turned down a snort of stronger stuff, and took her outside. We sat down under the trees and listened to the noise of people at peace. At the Grange affairs, they sort of put aside their likes and dislikes and to hear them you'd never suspect they were hog-poor and full of trouble.

"I don't see your brothers," Julie said.

"They'll likely show up," I told her. The music began again and I got up, pulling her to her feet. "That's too good to waste," I said.

The music seemed a little louder than it had been before and the dancing was a lot livelier, probably because some good whiskey had disappeared during that intermission. Julie and I whirled about and forgot about everything, except having a good time. By the time this set ended, people were beginning to notice that we always danced together and some talk was buzzing around. We didn't care, but wagging tongues can make up a lot of stories, and to cut some of them short, Julie left me and went over to where the ladies stood in matronly splendor.

I headed for Vince Randolf, who stood against the wall sipping his fruit punch. When I sided him, he said, "You're having a good time, Smoke."

"That's sure gospel."

"She's a nice girl," Randolf said. "Getting serious, Smoke?"

"Yep."

Randolf smiled. "That's nice to hear. Trouble comes and a man feels that there'll never be an end to it, then he sees a young couple in love and it restores something to him he thought he'd lost."

That the man had that kind of feelings sort of surprised me. Farmers are so poky and methodical that a man sometimes gets mixed up in his thinking about them. I looked around the room.

"I don't see Wade Everett," I said.

"Higgins stopped off before dark," Randolf said. "Wade told him he'd be here." He looked at me carefully for a moment. "There was good eatin' on that steer, Smoke. We'll remember that you gave it to him."

"Hell," I said, genuinely embarrassed. "I wish they'd stop talking about that."

"Sure," Randolf said. "Whatever you say, Smoke."

By chance I happened to be looking at the side door when Cord stepped in. He saw Ma and Edna sitting alone and went over immediately. He had a small box in his hand and he gave it to Ma. I watched as she ripped open the wrapper, then squealed with delight when she saw the imitation flowers. You know the kind, made of waxed paper. She grabbed Cord and pulled him down so she could kiss him. I could hear his laugh cutting under the talk and general babble.

He left them, walking toward us. He spoke to a few of the townsmen, but fended off any attempt to draw him into conversation. Vince Randolf's face was a study. He looked like he had business elsewhere, and yet pride held him motionless.

Cord had been traveling; dust powdered his clothes, although he had beat most of it off before coming inside. When he was close enough, he said, "Thought I'd find you here, Smoke." His eyes flicked to Vince Randolf. "Evenin', Randolf."

"Evenin'," Vince said and waited.

"Let's get out of here," he said to me. "Want to talk to you."

"I got a dance coming up with Julie," I told him.

His lips tightened a little; he never liked a family argument when the public was invited. He looked at Vince Randolf as if to tell him to move on, but the farmer held his place, his expression neutral.

"You seen Luther?" he asked.

"Nope. He left the place way before sundown. Rode toward Rindo's Springs."

"Well, he ought to stay at home more," Cord said.

"You been home?" I asked.

Cord shook his head. "Something wrong, Smoke?"

I shrugged. "Luther claimed he was leaving for good."

For an instant Cord just stared, then he slapped his thigh. "The fool!"

Vince Randolf edged his voice in. "Why a fool, O'Dare?"

"This is a family affair," Cord said, his voice intolerant. "Why don't you move on?"

About that time Bill Hageman saw Cord and excused himself, coming right over. He plucked his sack tobacco from his shirt pocket and began manufacturing a cigarette. "You look like a man who's traveled," Bill said.

"Some," Cord admitted. "A man who travels learns things."

"Such as?"

Cord looked at Vince Randolf, then at Bill Hageman. "Have you been to Rindo's Springs lately?"

"I never go there," Bill said. "The town's about folded."

"But Heck Overland hangs on," Cord said. "I took a look around the old loading pens. They've been used from time to time."

Bill Hageman took the cigarette from his mouth. "Go on, Cord. This is interesting."

"I started out combing the gullies," Cord said. "Nothing there except old tracks. But they all lead to Rindo's Springs and those old holding pens. The way I figure it, whoever is rustling our stock holds a few head in the gullies until he gets four or five. Heck flags the train and they load."

"Wasn't your brother heading for Rindo's Springs?" Randolf asked.

The look Cord gave him was enough to knock him over, but Randolf held his ground and returned stare for stare. "Don't jump to any conclusions," Cord said flatly.

"I won't," Randolf said. "I just know how to add two and two and get four, that's all."

"This is no time to go off half-cocked," Bill said quickly. "Cord, did you get any idea who's been pushing out stock?"

"No. Overland wasn't around. But I guess it would be easy enough to bait a trap."

"This is the time to telegraph for that marshal," Hageman said. "Cord, be sensible now. I don't know what this is about Luther going to Rindo's Springs, but to play it safe, you ought to call in the law."

"That's out," Cord said. "And I've told you why."

"I'd hate to think we took it on ourselves to hang the wrong man," Hageman said. "And that can happen easy enough, Cord."

"You're acting like a woman," Cord said. He looked at Vince Randolf. "Someone in this hall is a cattle rustler and has been stealing Bill and me blind. I want it passed around that I mean to catch that man."

"Does that go for Luther too?" Randolf asked easily.

You have to give him credit; he didn't scare easy. Cord looked like he was about to beat Randolf over the head with his pistol, but he held himself back. "Get this straight, Randolf: Luther's on the peck over something, but he'll be back. And when he gets here, I'm going to let him kick that insinuation down your throat."

There was no telling how far this argument would have developed if the preacher hadn't rung his little hand bell and announced that the box lunches would now be raffled off for charity. Now there wasn't a woman in that hall, save Ma and Edna, who didn't have a box up there on that table, and a man on the floor ready to bid for it. Cord frowned; he wasn't a man who liked his business interrupted, but then, he wasn't a man who liked to pass up his pleasures either.

The way this raffle went, the man who bid on the box, got the girl too, or at least a few dances and a sit-down under the trees. The dancing didn't worry me too much because I could keep an eye on Cord then, but that sit-down under the trees worried me plenty.

I tried to ease away, but Cord hung on like a wood tick. Having arrived late, he had no way of knowing which was Julie's lunch, but he knew that I knew. And he knew I wouldn't let it slide by without bidding either. All he'd have to do was wait it out and then top any bid I made.

I let the first few boxes go by without opening my mouth, then when I saw a pretty one come up, I bid a dollar. Cord snapped up the bait and went to two.

I dallied around a dollar and thirty-five cents, was raised to three and suddenly let him have it. Everyone cheered and Cord looked as pleased as a well-fed coon. That is, until he saw Huddlemeyer's daughter stand up. She was a solidly built six-footer, with shoulders like a section hand. Cord looked at me, stabbing me with his eyes, then smiled.

Hell, there wasn't anything else he could do.

Me? I was feeling as smug as a Wall Street bull completing a million-dollar merger, and sinking all my enemies at the same time. I played the basket-buying for all it was worth, knowing that Cord had promised to put me in my place where Julie was concerned, so he didn't dare pass up a chance that I was bidding on her basket.

I picked on one with a pink ribbon, edged him up to four and a half, then dropped it in his lap. Turned out to be a half-breed, the daughter of one of the railroad men. Again everyone cheered and the preacher said, "Dog me, Cord, but you're whoopin' it up tonight."

There weren't many folks in that hall who knew what was going on between me and Cord, but a few did. Julie for one. When I glanced at her, her eyes were shining and all for me, and they gave me the courage I needed to go on with this. And I think Vince Randolf guessed; he was a sharp man disguised in bib overalls and a bland expression. There was admiration in his glance, and I could forget how much I was sweating and what would happen afterward.

To make it short, I boxed Cord five times. I filled up his dance book with tall ones, fat ones, old ones, and anyone he hated on sight. Not a pretty one in the bunch, and save Huddlemeyer's girl, and the railroad man's breed daughter, they were all over forty, which is danged old out here.

I'd never seen Cord beat before; it wasn't pretty to watch. He looked like he was going to hit me then and there, but he didn't. He just whirled and rammed his way through the crowd and went outside to cool off.

When Julie's box came up, I gave five dollars for it, to show her I wasn't a piker, then went over to where she stood. She linked her arm in mine and gave me the kind of look women give their men just before they send them out to slay the giant.

"You were wonderful, Smoke. And I was wrong; you are your own man. You gave Cord a licking, the hardest kind for him to take."

"Yeah," I said, "and I may have to take one myself."

"No," she said. "I don't think Cord would ever fight you, Smoke."

To tell you the truth, I didn't dope that one out at the time; I was interested in the lunch and the sit-down under the trees. We went outside. Cord was standing on the porch smoking a cigarette. He looked at me as we went by and after we'd gone on ten feet or so, he said, "I want to talk to you, Smoke."

"Some other time," I said.

"I mean now."

I disengaged Julie's arm and turned around so that I faced him. "I guess you didn't hear me," I said. My heart was trying to knock its way out of my chest, but he didn't know that. We looked at each other for a moment, then Cord snubbed out his cigarette.

"All right," he said. "Some other time." He turned on his heel and went back inside.

I let out my breath with a long sigh. Sweat stood boldly on my forehead. Julie said, "Didn't I tell you, Smoke?"

This was beyond me and I was halfway afraid to question it. We sat down beneath a tree where the night shadows were thickest. I had the box lunch so I opened it, passing a sandwich and the bottle of coffee to Julie.

"I never seen him back down before, Julie. Never."

"Perhaps he's never faced up to a man before." I thought she was joking, but she wasn't, and I sat there, eating in silence, trying to figure this out, but there was no solution. Cord just wasn't acting normal tonight, that was all.

12

The dance started again, but we didn't go in immediately. The night was too nice to leave.We listened to the music and once I saw Cord wheel by with Huddlemeyer's daughter. The door was open and I got a good look. They danced stiffly, without grace, two thoroughly disenchanted people with nothing in common save their destination, and each hardly able to wait until they arrived.

A wagon pulled in from Main Street and I looked around, surprised to see Wade Everett's wife. She had the children with her and was in such a hurry that she didn't bother to tie the team. When she went inside I got up, pulling Julie with me. We walked toward the side door and before we stepped inside, the music had stopped, a deep hush falling over the hall.

People were standing about like wax statues in a museum. Cord was in the middle of the floor, his arm still around Huddlemeyer's daughter. Vince Randolf and the other farmers were backed against the refreshment table.

I looked at Wade Everett's wife. She was dirty and tears had washed pale streaks along her cheeks. Her eyes were on Cord and she trembled.

"Murderers! I found him! Found him after you'd hung him!"

The chatter started like a nest of squirrels arguing over a winter's supply of nuts. Cord slowly disengaged himself from Huddlemeyer's daughter while the preacher came forward, putting his arm around Mrs. Everett's shoulder and making soothing sounds with his lips. Someone brought out a chair and the preacher got her to sit down. He brought order; they were in the habit of listening to him.

"What is this, daughter? Calm yourself and tell us so we can understand."

Vince Randolf had the remedy, a belt of whiskey disguised in a glass of punch. Mrs. Everett drank it, coughed a bit, but finally seemed more composed. She twisted her hands together, her face distorted as she fought to get the words out.

"My man didn't come in this evenin'," she said. "Me an' Lige, that's m'oldest, went to look for him. We found him hanging in the barn. Dead."

The preacher had a tough time calming everyone; they all wanted to talk at once. I was shocked and even yet could hardly believe this; I liked Wade Everett since I'd come to know him better.

"Suicide?" Vince Randolf asked this in his calm voice.

She turned to look squarely at him. "If it had been suicide, there'd have been a box or somethin' for him to've jumped off of. But there wasn't nothin'. He was hoisted up there." Then her eyes whipped to Cord and bit in deep. "You killed him!"

"I didn't kill him," Cord said so quietly that he convinced nearly everyone. "Mrs. Everett, if he was murdered, I didn't do it."

"You hated him! You hate all us farmers!" She was beginning to cry again.

Cord frowned. "Hate? Not that. I had little use for you, I admit, but I don't hate any man enough to kill him."

She saw me out of the corner of her eye and suddenly all the blame and outrage was directed at me. "You!" This was an accusation in itself. "Oh, you cattlemen are smart. Comin' around with your talk. Givin' us meat so's you could come back later and have a ready excuse for killin' my man for rustlin'."

"What meat?" Cord asked. He was looking at me.

"I gave them a steer," I said. "They were getting low."

Vince Randolf frowned. "You didn't know about this, O'Dare?"

"Hell no!" Cord snapped. "There seems to be a lot going on I don't know about."

"You came in late," Randolf said. "You say you were at Rindo's Springs."

"Is this a trial?" Cord asked. He whipped around and looked at Bill Hageman. "You're cattle, Bill. Where were you?"

"I was asking you, O'Dare," Vince said.

Cord bit his lip, then said, "Heck Overland will swear that I didn't leave Rindo's Springs until well after dark. I'd been there all afternoon."

"You told us before that Overland wasn't there," Randolf pointed out.

"Damn it! I had my reasons." He blew out his breath and gained some control that way. Then he looked at Mrs. Everett. "This ain't the time or place, but when someone needs help, they need it regardless. Your man didn't have a nickel. How are you going to get along?"

"I'd take no charity from you!"

"This ain't charity," Cord said. "I'll give you three hundred for rights to your place. That's train fare out of here with some to eat on until you find something better."

She stared at Cord, while an angry murmur ran through the crowd. Then she spat on his boot; that was her answer and she couldn't have given him a plainer one.

"I was only trying to help," he said and turned toward the side door.

"Just a minute," Vince Randolf said. "We haven't talked about Luther yet."

Cord turned back. "And we won't, Randolf. When Luther comes back, he can talk for himself. Now if there's nothing else . . ."

"There is," Randolf said flatly. "We're going to telegraph for the law, O'Dare. We don't intend

161

to have a man killed and do nothing about it."

"Can't we handle this ourselves?" Cord asked.

"No," Randolf told him. "Perhaps Everett was the rustler; that's what you're thinking, but killing him that way is wrong."

"Be careful what you say about me," Cord warned. "I'm clear of this and I can prove it."

"You'll have your chance," Randolf promised and we stood there while Cord walked out.

I didn't want to look at Ma or Edna. Afraid to, I guess. Whatever friendliness had been circulating soon vanished and once again there were hostile people arrayed against each other; farmers against cattlemen, with the Hagemans and the O'Dares standing alone.

Bill came over, his thin face grave. "Damned lot of trouble here, Smoke."

"More'n I ever seen before," I admitted. I wasn't sure who was friend or foe now and it gave me an uneasy feeling.

"You take Julie home," Bill said. "I'll see that your Ma and Edna get started."

"What about you?"

Bill scratched his jaw. "I'll stay in town, I guess. Vince Randolf and I were fairly friendly once. The man may listen to me." He pulled out his hunting-case watch and popped the lids. "Ten to twelve. Vince will likely send the telegram within the hour, and the marshal will take the seven-o-nine in the morning. I want to be here when he arrives."

"Who the hell do you think did this, Bill?" I just had to ask, even a man who didn't know any more about it than I did.

He shook his head. "Cord said he was with Heck Overland. He wouldn't lie." He looked steadily at me and there was regret in his expression. "I'm thinking of Luther. And I guess there's others here who're thinking too."

That included me, for I knew Luther. He'd jumped Everett once already for nothing, or at least something that Everett had no part of. Now I wondered, and hated myself for doing it.

"We'd better go," Julie said.

She was right; there was nothing to be gained by staying, but quite possibly a lot of harm. The farmers were as hostile a looking bunch of people as I'd ever seen. Give them any kind of reason and they wouldn't hesitate to change their minds and settle for a little grass-roots justice, without the formality of a trial.

We went out to the buggy and I lifted Julie in, then untied the team and headed out of town. Now that I was leaving, I could look around with a little objectivity and be awed by what a crime can do to people. Friend now doubted friend and every glance was one of suspicion. A man could reasonably wonder who would be next.

Julie was inclined to silence, but she finally spoke. "It could even have been Bill, Smoke. Have you thought of that?"

"Yes," I said. "Only it doesn't fit Bill. He doesn't have a reason."

"You're wrong there," she said. "He has as good a reason as the O'Dares. We need land, Smoke. If a jury blamed Luther or Cord, you'd lose the home place and Bill could take it for little or nothing." She raised her hands and rubbed her face. "What am I saying, Smoke? Has the seed of suspicion gotten into me too?"

"We've got to believe," I said. "Julie, don't let this come in to bust us up."

"No," she said. "I don't want that, Smoke. We have to have faith."

That was sure the truth, but when you need it most, you'll find it the hardest to come by. The drive to Julie's seemed long and very tiresome and we were both a little glad when it ended. I put the team and buggy away for her, then borrowed a horse so I could get home.

She waited on the porch and when my good night sounded a little stiff, came into my arms with a rush, holding me like she was afraid I'd vanish if she let go. The feel of her lips on mine carried the same promise and thrill they had earlier, but it failed somehow to cut through my troubled thoughts. And I knew she was affected the same way.

"I'd better stay on the home place for a few days," I said.

"Come back when you can," she whispered. "Or I'll come to you."

I mounted bareback and rode out, not stopping at the river. After splashing across, I let the horse run, and once home, turned him into the corral with the others.

The house was bright with lamplight. Ma and Edna were home; the buggy was parked by the porch, forgotten. And Luther was home; his horse stood weary and three-footed, head down. As I crossed the yard, I could hear Cord's angry voice.

Ma and Edna were in the kitchen and Ma was crying, with Edna trying to comfort her. Cord paced up and down the parlor, his face like a Kansas twister, dark and forbidding and full of danger. I looked at Luther, who sat like a whipped hound, his face dejected, eyes cast to the worn rug.

Cord gave me no more than a glance, then went on with his lecture. "A damn snot-nosed kid, that's what you are! Something don't suit you, you run off, then come crying back. Where did you go after you left Overland's place?"

"I told you," Luther said wearily. "Just riding around. Jesus, you act like I done it!"

"Well, somebody did," Cord said. He glared at me. "Not you; anybody'd know that. You don't even like to spur your horse."

"You can take your spurs out of me right now," I said, "and your mad to somebody else."

Cord's eyes got wide. "Well, now, you just have

your little heart set on crossing me tonight, don't you?"

"Ain't we got enough trouble?" I asked. "You got to make more?"

Cord slapped his thighs and went on pacing. Finally he stopped and stood in front of Luther. "Now listen to me. I know you wouldn't do a thing like hanging a man, but those farmers don't know it. O'Dare is a filthy word with them right now, and of all the damned times to go wandering around the country, this has to be it."

"I wasn't anywhere near Everett's place," Luther said. "As God is my witness, I swear it."

"All right, all right," Cord said, waving his hand impatiently. "I believe you, but we've got to do something. Randolf wasn't fooling when he said he'd send for the marshal. There's going to be a stink over this."

"Ain't someone going to think about Everett's widow?"

Cord flipped his head around. "Smoke, you've got enough to worry about right here. I'm going to have to hire a lawyer before I'm through. You know what they cost?"

"Maybe three hundred dollars?" I asked. "The price of a half-section?"

He swore loud enough to attract Ma and Edna, and he started for me. Always before I'd stood and taken my licking, but this time was different, the turning point or something. When he got within reach, I grabbed up a vase from the table and broke it across his forehead. Cord went down to one knee, bracing himself with his hands. He wasn't out, but he was seeing the prettiest stars a man could see.

Ma rushed over and flung her fat arms around him. "Son! God, son, are you hurt?"

She helped him up, her plump hands patting his face, brushing back that lock of hair. Cord sort of staggered a little when Ma helped him into a chair and he sat for a few minutes with his head held between his hands. Ma looked at me as though she was ashamed I'd ever been born.

"Smoke, the devil's in you, striking Cord that way!"

Walking out on people isn't my habit, but I'd suddenly had a crawful. I wheeled and stomped down the hall and slammed the door of my room behind me. A moment later I looked up as Edna opened the door and stepped inside, closing it gently.

"So you're revolting, Smoke."

"Is that a cuss word?"

She smiled faintly. "No. It might be a compliment." She came over and sat on the bed beside me. "Smoke, what's happening to us?"

"We're coming apart," I said. "The O'Dare glue ain't as good as we thought."

"It was bad enough when Cord lit into Luther.

Now you." She put her hand over mine. "I saw you with Julie tonight. You haven't quarreled?" I shook my head. "Then that's good. I wish I could believe like that."

"What do you mean?" I asked.

"I mean, I wish I knew Luther better. Believing would be easier then." She paused. "Smoke, that day he came home dusty, he told me what really happened."

"Well," I said, "he never could keep his mouth shut."

"That doesn't matter now," Edna said. "If there's a trial, and there surely seems to be one brewing, can you put your hand on the Bible and lie for Luther?"

I'd never thought of that and now that I had, I didn't want to consider it further. But I had to; there was no way out. "I could skip the country," I said.

"And be blamed for that man's death? That's no good and you know it."

"What then?"

"I don't know." Her voice was listless. "Smoke, I love my husband. Really love him. But I can see how bad this is going to look in court."

"But maybe it won't get to court," I said. "Edna, maybe something will turn up, the real killer caught."

"That's a slim hope, Smoke, and you know it." She stood up and stepped to the door. "I want you to help my husband. For me. Will you promise me that?"

I nodded. "Sure, Edna. Luther didn't do it. There's no evidence to prove that he did. Not a damned bit."

"Let's hope you're right," she said and stepped out.

13

Later I lay on my bed, staring at the ceiling, trying to find the straight of it all, but I could only see frazzled ends. There was no use denying that Luther had had a fight with Wade Everett; Everett's wife would testify to that and I'd have to back her story. Right then I wished that I was the world's worst liar, someone who couldn't be believed under oath. But I wasn't. Whatever set of principles I had was cemented pretty solid and there wasn't much I could do about them.

Sleep refused to come to me; I tried for an hour. Cord, Ma, Luther and Edna had all gone to bed and the house was quiet. I slipped out and walked across the yard to the barn. I saddled my pony and led him clear of the place before mounting. Dawn wasn't far away and the wind was starting to die down. Being in no particular hurry, I eased toward Wade Everett's place, but didn't go too near. Skirting it, I rode on toward Vince Randolf's.

There wasn't any real purpose to this wandering, and I began to understand how Luther could have killed so much time just easing along, working out his problems. For a time I dismounted and hunkered down, and then I got restless again and mounted.

About a mile away from Randolf's place I saw a light come on. Someone was up and getting breakfast. I walked the horse, not taking any pains about being quiet, and suddenly the back door opened and Randolf popped out. He didn't stand with his back to the light but stepped aside and covered himself with the predawn blackness.

"Who's there?"

"Smoke O'Dare! I come to talk!"

"The hell you have!" Randolf yelled, then a bright blossom of orange bloomed momentarily and the echo of the shot split the silence, rolling across the prairie. I never did know where that bullet went, but I didn't hang around to find out where the next one would go.

My pony was pretty fast on the start and the spurs convinced him that I wanted to go. Randolf didn't shoot again and I was out of range in a hurry. About a mile from the place, I settled back to a walk and quieted a case of the shakes.

The seeds of suspicion, it seemed, had evidently flourished in the usually level-headed Vince Randolf.

Returning to the home place was the last thought in my mind, yet I had no other place to go. The dawn finally arrived, along with the brassy sun and the promise of early heat. I edged clear around Higgins' place, and Mooney's, on the chance that they might be able to shoot a little straighter in the daylight.

When I passed Everett's soddy, I stopped for a look. Not a breath of anything stirred and I figured that this was fitting, seeing that death had so recently visited there. Everett's wagon was not there and I figured that his wife and children had stayed on in town.

Don't know why, but I felt drawn to the place. I eased in, dismounting in the yard. After tying my horse to the fence, I walked toward the barn, stopping before I got there. There was a fresh mound near the south wall, Wade Everett's grave, and I could just see his wife digging that, weeping and digging until finally it was finished, and maybe some of the weeping too.

I went in the barn for a look around. Everett didn't have much, either in the way of tools or fodder. And he never did get the roof finished. A look at the rafters pointed out the one on which he had been hung; the wood was worn slick where the rope had chafed while he thrashed about.

And then I found the rope.

Not just any kind of rope, like you would find on a well bucket. This was a cattleman's rope, yet it was more than that too. It was a rope that pointed a finger, just as surely as if Wade Everett were doing it from the grave. For the rope belonged to Luther O'Dare!

Quickly I opened my shirt and stuffed it inside

as though afraid God would look down and identify it too.

I stood there, letting my doubts and suspicions have their way with me, and, forgive me, I made up as good a case against Luther as any prosecutor could have. Luther couldn't have had a better motive: anger. And a desire to strike back, to revenge himself.

Cord had always said that he'd hang the man found with one of our steers; suspicion would fall Cord's way and Luther knew that. The rest? His absence and the rope would make a definite impression on a jury.

Staying any longer at Wade Everett's place was out of the question; I mounted and swung away, not toward the home place, but toward Rindo's Springs. That was the most miserable ride I ever took. After a while I removed Luther's rope from beneath my shirt, coiled it, and hung it on my saddle.

The flatlands ended a few miles this side of Rindo's Springs and the land rose in shallow hummocks, deepening beyond where horizon and sky met. Ten years before, Rindo's Springs had been a lively little town, a mecca for all the cattlemen running stock on the land leased from the Cherokee, or any other breed of Indian who cared to put his mark on a paper as worthless as he was. But the leases were broken and men moved away, back to Texas, or on to Wyoming, and Rindo's Springs just kind of dried up with no one except Heck Overland staying on.

The town lay in a small swale with the railroad cutting past the north edge. Two deserted streets and a dozen or so buildings sagging against each other. Weeds grew in the middle of the main street, and the wind had drifted the dust completely over the rotted boardwalk in spots.

The only place in the whole town that was open for business was Heck Overland's String of Pearls, the saloon setting on the northeast corner of Race and Bad Luck Streets. Deserted towns are not my dish and I let the pony singlefoot down toward the saloon, all the time keeping my head moving from left to right and back again. When I pulled up in front of Overland's place, he came out; riders stopping here were rare and worth a first-hand look.

He peered at me from beneath his shaggy brows. "Ain't you the young O'Dare boy?"

"Smoke," I said. "We don't see much of you in Ponca City, Mr. Overland."

"Like it here," Overland said. He was a huge man, nearly six-two; shaggy beard and unwashed shirt rolled to the elbows to expose red flannel underwear made me think of a derelict cast up on some forgotten beach. "We don't see much of you O'Dares either," Heck Overland said. " 'Ceptin' Luther." He turned toward the sagging saloon doors. "Come in. You must be thirsty."

The inside was as rundown as the exterior. Dust covered the poker tables and the piano near the stage hadn't given out a melody in years. I sort of expected to see a few ghosts come out on the stage and dance, in memory of the old days.

Overland went behind his bar and placed a bottle and glass where I could get at them. He poured and shoved one my way. "Here's a tear," he said, "providing you got something to cry about."

I downed mine and nearly choked. I've heard that whiskey gets better with age, but better at what? This went down as smooth as a newly sharpened cross-cut saw. Overland seemed immune to his own whiskey for he downed his drink without batting an eye.

Then he looked at me real steady and said, "What're you doing here, Smoke?"

"Ridin'," I said. "Been meaning to get over this way for some time."

"Why?"

A blunt question can sure stop a man cold. I fooled around with my whiskey glass and wondered what I should say. "Was Cord here yesterday?"

"He was," Overland said. "We played blackjack most of the afternoon. Was well after dark before he left. Nine, I'd say."

I bit my lip, afraid to ask any more. Heck Overland saved me the trouble. "Luther was here too. Left around six or seven. Closer to seven, I think."

"Anything bothering him?"

Overland's eyes got round and careful and full of secrets. "What do you mean, bothering him?"

"Well, he left home sort of riled. I wondered if he and Cord had words."

"Cord told him a thing or two," Overland said. He scratched his whiskers. "Let me see now. Luther was on the peck about something. Lit into Cord. A lot I didn't understand. Damned foolishness, if you ask me. Cord backed him down and Luther stormed out of here." Overland carefully refilled his shot glass. "Something wrong, Smoke?"

"Wade Everett was killed last night around dark."

"Too bad," Overland said. "I didn't know the man at all. Never had truck with farmers."

"There's going to be a lot of trouble," I said. "The farmers have sent to Oklahoma City for a marshal."

"Oh?" Overland's tone was careful. "He going to investigate the killin'?"

"And the rustling too," I said. "Cord mentioned that you've shipped a few head from here, time to time."

"Might have," Overland said. He placed his hands on the edge of the bar. "Wouldn't ask too many questions, was I you. Might get some answers you wouldn't like."

I couldn't have agreed more, but there is something in a man that makes him search for the truth, even when it hurts the most. "Why don't you try me?"

"Well," Overland said, "you're an O'Dare and I guess blood's thicker than water. I've shipped a few head now and then for Luther. Young heifers, mostly. Got a brother-in-law who's a brakie on the railroad. Just set out a lantern and the train'd stop." He put out his hand and took me by the arm. "Don't look so puke-faced, boy. Surely you knew . . ."

"I didn't know!" I yelled. "And Cord all the time threatening to hang . . ."

"Whoa, whoa there," Overland said softly. "Cord knew, toward the last. That talk was a smoke to cover up what he knew." He gave me a shake. "Now you go on home and leave this to Cord. There ain't nothin' going to happen that he can't handle."

"Yeah," I said. "Cord will handle everything. He always has."

I turned and walked to the door and outside, but I couldn't seem to come out of the shock. Overland came to the porch while I mounted. Then Overland said, "When you see Cord, tell him to come over."

"What for?"

"Never you mind," Overland said. "You just tell him that him and I have some business to discuss. He'll understand."

"All right," I said.

"And don't forget," Overland cautioned. "I'll be expectin' him, you understand?"

I nodded and turned out of town. I tried to think, but that seemed impossible. All I was aware of was the terrible knowledge I held, that my own brother was a cattle rustler and a killer. A man can doubt his sanity at a time like that. All the things he believes turn to nothing and his understanding of another turns to a worthless, meaningless jumble.

On my saddle was the rope that had done the ugly job; I could hide it or destroy it. But I knew that I wouldn't help Luther that way. The marshal would be a professional man hunter and my tracks were in Wade Everett's yard. There would be questions and I could lie, but not good enough to fool a man trained to detect lies. The trail would lead to Rindo's Springs and Heck Overland would tell what he knew, and then I'd have to stand by while the law sprung the trap on Luther.

14

The sun had swung around to mid-afternoon before I neared the home place, but I didn't stop. To go in that house and face Luther now was out of the question. I rode on toward the river, paused there for a time, then crossed over to Bill Hageman's place.

He had just ridden in a short time before; his horse, tied to the hitch rack in front of the porch, was still sweaty. Julie heard me crossing the yard and came out. I dismounted slowly and tied up.

"Smoke," she cried, "what's wrong?"

I just shook my head and stepped into the shade. "Bill home?"

"He's inside. Smoke, what happened?"

I took her arm and we went into the house. Bill was in the kitchen, stripped to the waist, and washing the refuse of a sleepless night from his eyes. He turned and looked at me, then put the towel aside.

"Sit down, Smoke." He pulled a chair away from the table and I sort of dropped in it, as though my legs no longer wanted to support my weight.

"The marshal get here?"

"An hour ago. They sent Bud Ledbetter.

Couldn't have picked a better man." He scraped back another chair and sat down across from me. "What's the matter with you, Smoke? I've never seen you looking so peaked before."

And I'd never felt this way before either, so I told him everything, the whole, rotten story, about the rope and what Heck Overland had said and the quarrel Luther had had with Everett. I told him because I was lost and confused and couldn't think of an answer to any of it.

Julie watched me, not saying anything. Bill never took his eyes off my face and when I finished, he shook out his sack of tobacco and rolled a cigarette. Somehow this familiar act calmed me, gave me an anchor with which to snub my troubles.

"This looks bad for Luther," he said quietly. "What are you going to do about it, Smoke?"

"I don't know," I admitted. "What can I do, Bill? Tell me and I'll do it."

He shook his head. "At a time like this, a man has to do what he thinks is right. I can't help you, Smoke. Julie can't help you either."

"But what would you do?"

"I don't know," Bill said. "It all depends on what a man is inside. How deep does his sense of right and wrong go?"

"Good God, you're talking about my brother!"

Bill nodded. "He's Cord's brother too. What would Cord do about it?"

"Cover for him," I said without hesitation. "He must have been covering for him all along. It's the only reason he could have had for egging you into a fight, trying to keep everybody from looking too closely at the O'Dares." I placed my face in my hands. "I can't carry this load, Bill. Maybe Cord can, but I'm not heavy enough."

"No one can carry it for you," Bill Hageman said. "Smoke, there comes a time in every man's life when he has to stand alone, if he has integrity. Without it, he'll fall, and once he's fallen, he'll never be the same again." He got up and put his hand on my shoulder. "Julie and I are going to forget what you said here, if that's the way you choose to play it, Smoke. You do what you feel is right, and think about it carefully."

I looked at him. "Turn him in?"

"I can't tell you," Bill said and went down the hall.

Julie waited; she even came around to my side and put her arm around me. She didn't say anything to help me; there was nothing she could say. This was my time to rise or fall as a man, and it was a terrible decision to make, against one's own brother.

Her voice was soft when she said, "I love you, Smoke, really love you."

How I'd wanted to hear her say that! I looked at her. "But you'd love me a lot less if I failed you now, wouldn't you?"

"No," she said. "A man can only be what he is. He can't rise very far above that, no matter how hard he tries."

I stayed in Bill Hageman's kitchen for almost an hour, and if ever Jehovah and Old Scratch wrestled for a man's soul, they sure did over mine. Julie stayed with me, remaining silent, but lending an infinite strength just by being there. The kitchen clock ticked off the minutes, then finally I stood up and walked out of the house. She followed me to the porch where Bill waited.

After untying my horse and swinging up, I said, "What kind of a fella is Bud Ledbetter? Easy to talk to? Because what I got to say is going to come hard."

Julie suddenly put her hands over her face and began to cry, but with relief, I knew. Bill threw away his cigarette and stepped off the porch. His voice was very soft. "You're the tallest man I've seen in a spell of Sundays, Smoke. I'll ride along with you, if you want."

"I'll go this one alone," I said and wheeled away, taking the Ponca City road.

Of the hundred-odd times I'd traveled that road, the one I'll always remember is the one I want to forget the most. I tried riding fast, half afraid that if I took my time, I'd alter my decision. But I didn't. Once my mind was made up, it stayed that way, and the hurt was something I was going to have to live with the rest of my life.

When I got to town I stopped at the end of the street, hardly able to believe what I saw. Every farmer in our part of the country was in town, and armed. They moved about with a grim restlessness. When I rode down that street, every eye was on me, and I imagine the impulse to kill me was strong in more than one man. I saw Vince Randolf standing in front of the hotel with a double-barreled shotgun in the crook of his arm and I pulled in, dismounting.

"I missed you the other night," Vince said evenly. "I'm sorry I did. Just want you to get that straight."

I looked at his frozen, friendless expression. His eyes reminded me of a friendly dog's after he has been unaccountably turned against. Was this the same man I had talked to? He looked the same, but he had changed overnight into something I hardly recognized.

"Mr. Randolf, where can I find the United States Marshal?"

"Inside," Randolf said. He stepped aside to let me pass.

The clerk looked at me uneasily. "Mr. Ledbetter? Room eight at the head of the stairs."

I went up, counting each step as though they led to the gallows. At number eight I knocked and a bass voice invited me in.

Bud Ledbetter was stretched out on the bed; he swung his feet to the floor as I closed the door. He was a small man, in his fifties, white-haired and his thick mustache had been time-bleached to match his mane. He had eyes as clear as glass marbles, yet there was warmth in the man; I felt it instinctively.

"You're not a farmer," he said evenly, "and since Hageman has no brothers, you must be an O'Dare."

"Smoke," I said. "Henry O'Dare."

"I'll call you Smoke," Ledbetter said, motioning toward a chair. "Care for a cigar?"

"No, sir." I waited until he put a match to his. "I've got to talk to you, sir."

"About the killing?"

"Yes, sir."

Ledbetter walked over to the window and looked out at the street. Cigar smoke wreathed his face, and he spoke without looking at me. "Those farmers down there aren't in a playful mood. Being a cattleman, you took a chance coming in here. Must have been important." He turned and looked at me. "Got something I ought to know?"

"Yes, sir. I have the rope that hung Wade Everett."

His expression remained inflexible. "Did you hang him, son?"

"No, and I ain't sure who did."

"Then how do you know about the rope?" His eyes held a deep interest, perhaps curiosity.

"Better tell me all about it," he said and sat down on the edge of the bed.

While I talked, he smoked his cigar to a sour stub, then kindled another one. My own voice sounded strange in my ears and I didn't leave out a thing. Ledbetter nodded now and then, or stroked his mustache, and twice pulled out his stem-winder and consulted it. He was a neatly dressed, gentle-mannered man, more like a hardware salesman than a famous marshal who had shot it out with quite a few bad ones.

When there was no more to tell, Ledbetter asked the question I was afraid I'd never be able to answer. "Why, Smoke?"

What was the answer? I went over to the window, where he had stood a short time before, and looked down into the street, studying the hostility there, the suspicion, and the men I no longer knew or understood. Finally I had an answer; I turned around and said, "Because we can't go on living like this, Marshal. We can't go on looking at each other and thinking things about each other. A man's better off dead than living like that. We either got to trust each other and get along, or we'll all end up bad."

"That is," Ledbetter said softly, "as good a reason as a man can have. But the price to you is high." He picked up his hat and squared it on his head. From his cloth satchel, he took a pearl-handled Frontier with a very short barrel and dropped it into his coat pocket. "Shall we go? I'll have to arrest Luther."

He would have gone alone, I know, but I had to go along with him, and that was the hardest of all, facing Cord and Ma and Edna. And Luther. Afterward I could run, but only after I'd faced them with what I'd done.

Vince Randolf stared at me when we stepped to the boardwalk. Bud Ledbetter paused for a moment, and said, "I'd like to see the rope now." He waited there while I went to my horse and brought it back.

Randolf crowded close for a look and the others moving along the walk sensed that something was up and began to gather around, making a ring of hostility. Bud Ledbetter was a smart man, and a careful one. He examined every inch of the rope, particularly where it had chafed over the rafter. Then he coiled it carefully and slipped it over his arm.

"What rope is that?" Vince Randolf asked.

"Evidence," Ledbetter said, looking carefully at Randolf.

"Is that the rope that was used to hang Everett?" He didn't wait for an answer, just singled me out with his hate and suspicion. "What are you doing with it? How did you get it if you didn't have a hand in killing Everett?"

A spark was all that was needed here and Randolf's voice provided it. The ring of suspicion became a vicious thing, pressing close. Someone struck me on the back of the neck and I fell into Ledbetter, not unconscious, but mad and wanting to strike back. Ledbetter was looking at Randolf, who had his shotgun level with the marshal's stomach.

"Put that up," Ledbetter said.

"We'll take care of this now," Randolf said. "Step out of the way, Marshal."

"Unless you surrender that weapon," Ledbetter said, "I'll have to take it away from you by force."

Had Ledbetter shouted, I'm sure that he'd have been a dead man, but the calmness of his voice carried a conviction beyond doubt; the crowd began to ease back, afraid that Randolf would do something foolish for which they would be blamed. I had never seen Randolf's face so set, or his eyes so blankly wild. Ledbetter took a step, his hand outstretched.

"You're a man of peace, farmer. Do you want mob law?"

"I want a murderer hung!"

"So you want to become one to hang one?" Ledbetter took another step. He had three to go; I wouldn't have traded places with him for all the gold in the Guthrie bank.

"Don't make me use violence," Randolf said. "I don't want to."

"Of course you don't want to," Ledbetter said,

taking another step. "You want justice, not murder to wipe out murder." His hand wasn't two feet from the muzzle of that shotgun, but I wondered if he'd ever make it.

I couldn't tell whether Randolf would shoot or not. There was no figuring the man now, no telling what he would do, worked up the way he was. But Ledbetter must have known. Those lessons learned through the years while facing dangerous men must have told him more about Randolf than I would ever know. He took that last step, pushed the muzzle toward the ground and gently pulled it from Vince Randolf's grasp. Without altering his expression, he broke open the gun, kicked out the two buckshot loads and handed the empty gun back.

To me, he said, "Shall we go now?"

A lane just opened up and we stepped into the saddle. Ledbetter paused to look at the silent crowd on the hotel porch. "I may be coming back into town shortly with a prisoner. It would grieve me if I was forced to use violence to protect him." He singled out Vince Randolf, putting the weight of responsibility squarely on his shoulders. "See that you keep your friends quiet."

We rode down the main street together, like we were in no particular hurry. Finally Ledbetter said, "Did that fellow hurt you when he hit you from behind?"

"No," I said. My neck ached but I didn't think it was worth mentioning.

"Men just have to strike out at times," Ledbetter said. "A wise man never holds it against them." He rode for a time in silence, then began to ask me questions about myself, and Cord. His voice was always soft-pitched; I doubt that he was capable of shouting. Yet he had a way of drawing a man out, of getting at the truth, and what was more important, he gathered together those high points of information which gave him an understanding as to why a man did what he did.

The closer we got to the home place, the deeper my dread became. Bud Ledbetter understood this, but said nothing about it or by manner indicated that he was aware of it. When we could clearly see the house in the distance, he said, "I'll do the talking, Smoke. Please keep out of any difficulty that might arise."

"Yes, sir."

He looked at me and smiled. "If there is any justice in the O'Dares, they'll not blame you for this."

He made it sound good, only I knew how it was going to be and all the noble ideals which had led me to this decision now fled and I felt as Judas must have felt before receiving his pieces of silver.

15

As we rode into the yard, Cord came to the barn door for his look. Then he hurried toward us as we dismounted by the back porch. "Where the hell have you been, Smoke?" His glance was intolerant when he turned it on Ledbetter. "Who the hell are you?"

"United States Marshal," Ledbetter said. He peeled back the cuff of his coat, revealing a small crescent of silver. Then he took Luther's rope from his saddle horn. "Can you identify this, Mr. O'Dare?"

Cord glanced at it briefly. "It belongs to Luther. What is this anyway?"

From inside the house came the tinkle of Ma's music box, an odd sound in the silence. Ledbetter said, "Is Luther at home?"

"He's sleeping," Cord said.

"Then I think we'd best go inside," Ledbetter suggested. He turned Cord by taking his arm. Cord didn't like this, but he opened the door and we stepped into the hot kitchen. Ma was bustling about, singing in a droning voice while the music box played. I stepped up to the table and closed the lid, bringing the waltz to a sudden conclusion.

Ma turned, surprised and a little displeased.

"I like that tune, Smoke." She opened the lid and I closed it again. Then she saw Ledbetter standing there. "Who are you?"

The marshal introduced himself, then said, "Would you wake your brother, Smoke."

Cord said, "I'll do it."

"I asked him," Ledbetter said. I went down the hall, feeling pretty sorry for myself. It wasn't bad enough that I had to turn him in, I had to wake him so he could be arrested. Edna had been in the room with Luther; she came out as I lifted my hand to knock.

"Who's in the kitchen?" she asked. "I heard voices."

"A marshal from Oklahoma City," I said. "Luther awake?"

"He's getting up," she said.

I waited for him and he came out a moment later, stuffing his shirttail into his waistband. "Better get into the kitchen," I said.

"Trouble?"

All I could do was to nod.

I followed Luther down the hall, ashamed to even look at him. Ledbetter was standing by the door, his face serene. Cord was moving about, goaded by an animal restlessness. Luther nodded to the marshal but said nothing.

"As a federal peace officer," Ledbetter said, "it is my duty to arrest you, Luther O'Dare, on suspicion of murder."

The silence was appalling; it was painful to the ears. Cord looked blank for a moment, then said, "What the hell do you mean, murder?"

"You yourself identified the rope," Ledbetter said. "It was found in Wade Everett's barn and I'm sure we can prove that it was used to hang Everett."

"Who found it?" Cord asked. "How did you get it?"

"I found it," I said. Didn't think I could get it out, but I had too much pride to let the marshal say it for me. "And I took it to town."

"You turned in your own brother!" Cord screamed this.

What happened then I can only give you in flashes; that's the way I saw it and remember it. Luther stared while Edna's face turned ugly. The veins on Cord's forehead stood out sharply; I recall nothing else about him in that moment.

Ma whined as though she had been struck a mortal blow, then whirled to the stove and flung a full pot of scalding coffee at me. I don't know how I ducked that, but I did, or almost did. I flung up an arm instinctively and had it burned from elbow to wrist.

She tried to get at me then, like a crazy woman, and I guess she was. Ledbetter kept blocking her with his body, butting her back, trying to calm her with his soothing voice. Cord had his fists clenched and was shouting at me. "You filthy Judas! I ought to kill you here and now!"

And I think he might have if Bud Ledbetter hadn't stopped him. He put his hand in his coat pocket and Cord knew there was a gun there.

Ma was crying; her face was twisted and unrecognizable. "Oh, what have I raised?" she wailed. "I should have killed you at birth rather than you should do this to me." Before the marshal could stop her, she raked me across the face with her fingernails and then she spit on me. I didn't fight her; I just stood there with the acid of her loathing running down my cheek.

Bud Ledbetter said, "Better come along, Luther."

"He's not going," Cord said flatly. "Don't try and take him either, Marshal."

"I'll take him," Ledbetter said. "Easy or hard, he'll go along with me."

Ma whirled to Cord. "Don't let him go, Cord! You've held us together all these years! Don't let him take my boy now!"

"Step out here, Luther," Ledbetter said. "If you're innocent, you'll have every chance to prove it."

"I *am* innocent," Luther said in a stunned voice. "Before God, I swear it." He stepped around Edna, fending off her grasping hands.

"I've got a gun in my room," Cord said. "Don't make me defend my brother."

Ledbetter now had Luther by the arm and was backing toward the door, while from the yard

193

came the drum of horses approaching. I kept watching Cord, standing so stiff and angry; then I was out on the porch and Ledbetter and Luther were coming out.

Cord wheeled; he was going after his gun and Ledbetter knew it. "Go to the barn," he said quickly. "Get a horse for Luther and never mind the saddle."

I whipped around to do as he asked, then saw Julie and Bill Hageman dismounting. Bill had a rifle and Ledbetter gave them a quick, uncertain glance.

"They're friends," I said. "Bill, we need backing here."

"You've got it," he said and stood there, his rifle held lax in his hands. I ran on to the barn, threw a bridle on the first horse I came to and led him back. Cord was out on the porch now, his .44 Smith & Wesson in his hand. He and Ledbetter were having a staring match, with Bill Hageman standing behind the marshal and a little to one side.

"Don't make me kill an officer of the law," Cord said. Ma and Edna crowded the doorway. Ma was wailing and Edna was trying to calm her.

Ledbetter said, "I'm not making you do anything, Mr. O'Dare. Get on that horse, Luther. You too, Smoke."

Luther hesitated, then flipped up. I climbed aboard my own mount and waited, my breath choked off. Ledbetter's hand was still in his pocket; he hadn't yet drawn his gun. He faced Cord without fear; I had never known another man to do that.

Glancing at Bill Hageman, Cord said, "Bill, I'll square this with you if you interfere."

"Then don't force me," Bill told him. "Cord, the law has to be served; no one man has the right to set up his own laws against it. If you shoot that pistol, you're a dead man. That's a promise." He spoke to Bud Ledbetter without looking at him. "Marshal, if you'd like, just get on your horse and ride out. I'll wait here a spell."

"We'll go together," Ledbetter said, "after he puts down his pistol."

There was no telling how this would have turned out if Ma hadn't rushed out and grabbed Cord's arm. "I don't want you killed!" she yelled. "You're my man, Cord, my grown-up man. I'd die without you! We'll get Luther back, Cord. But not if it means you harm!"

I waited, breath held, then the anger drained out of Cord, leaving him slack-bodied and sweating. He tossed his .44 into the dust and we turned, riding out of the yard together. Ledbetter never once looked back; that was the kind of nerve he had. But Bill Hageman did, and he kept his rifle handy in case Cord had a change of mind. Julie rode beside me, saying nothing.

At the road we stopped. Bill Hageman said, "If

you want a place to bunk, Smoke, our door's always open."

"I'll stay in town," I said. "I've been skunk-sprayed proper."

Ledbetter wanted to get on his way; we parted there and Julie and Bill crossed the river. I sided Luther; I felt that I had to. The marshal rode behind but he didn't seem like a man who ever worried about losing his prisoner.

"I had to do it, Luther," I said. "I just had to."

He looked at me then and of all the people who had a right to hate me the most, he was the man. But he didn't; I saw that immediately. "I guess you did what you believed was right, Smoke. And I envy you for that. Wish I could do what was right. You believe I hung Everett?"

"I don't know," I said. "Luther, you do some damn fool things sometimes. . . ."

"I didn't kill anyone," he said. "Hell, you know I couldn't kill anyone. Not hang a man." He paused. "That's my rope all right. Guess it looks bad, seeing as how I fought him like I did. But I was only taking my mad out on him, Smoke. That was all."

How can I tell how much I wanted to believe him? Yet how could I ignore his unpredictable nature, his facility for doing the foolish and unwise thing? Before, it never seemed to matter whether I believed him or not, but now that it did matter, I couldn't summon any faith.

Ponca City didn't have a jail so Marshal Ledbetter kept Luther in his room, handcuffing him to the iron bedstead at night. Ledbetter's suggestion to Vince Randolf reaped a fine harvest; the farmers remained orderly and even put up their weapons, impressed by the hasty arrest, and confident that they would soon get a just con-viction.

I took a room at the hotel, paying for it with the cattle money I still had in my pocket. The next day Cord drove Ma into town and Ledbetter allowed her to visit with Luther. Edna came in with them and did not go back to the home place. She rented a room so that she could be near her husband.

Ma didn't want to see me, or speak to me, but Cord came around. I was a little surprised, and very much afraid, when I opened my door and saw him standing by the window. He looked at my bandaged arm, the one Ma had scalded properly, then said, "I didn't think you'd mind my coming in to wait."

"Didn't know you wanted to come in," I said. "How's Ma?"

"Taking this pretty hard," he said. He was ill at ease and understandably so; I wasn't a very nice person to be around. Even the farmers felt that way. Sure, I'd smoked out their man for them, but still there was a bad taste in their mouths.

"Did you get a lawyer for Luther?" I asked.

"Sent a telegram off to Guthrie as soon as I came to town," Cord said. "Lawyers take money. How about handing over what you got from the cattle buyer?"

"Sure," I said, and gave it to him. He counted it, which was his way of telling me that he didn't consider me above stealing. "You're a hundred shy."

"I have to live too, or don't you think I deserve it?"

"I'm not mad at you now," Cord said. "Just hurt that you didn't come to me first. I'd have handled everything." He wiped his hand across his mouth. "I've worked hard to build up the home place, even after the damned government took every-thing away from me. We could have got Luther off if we'd stuck together. Together we could have sworn that he was at home when it happened. Now I've got to fight this out in court. Maybe we'll win and maybe we won't, but either way it's given the farmers an edge I never wanted them to have. You put the law on the side of a man, Smoke, and you're whipped. Given a little more time and this damned drought and I could have bought 'em all out."

This made me boil. "Is that all this means to you, land? Hell, don't you give a damn that Luther's been arrested for killing a man?"

"You're saying things you don't mean," Cord

said. "I've always thought of the family first. You know that."

"Have you? How? By buying Ma knick-knacks? By picking Luther's wife for him?"

"Everything I've done has been for you," Cord said flatly. His eyes got dull and dedicated and he acted real noble about it all. "Everything's been for the family. I've been a father to all of you. Everything you wanted. I don't deserve to be criticized for what I've done."

"What have you done? Made Luther into something he was never cut out to be? Made him say, 'yes, sir,' and 'no, sir,' and do everything you wanted?" I blew out an angry breath. "And you've leaned on me plenty, always making me do your share of the work while you chase all over the country."

"Is this the thanks I get for dedicating my life?" Cord asked. "I could have had a wife, but I've denied myself that because of the family. Is my reward a lot of smart talk?"

This made me laugh; a few weeks ago I wouldn't have dared, but everything had changed since then. "Don't hand me that I-could-have-got-married stuff. You couldn't stay with a woman three months without wantin' another. Hell, look at what you've done for us! Look at Ma, crawling around when you whisper. What do you carry that big gun for if it ain't to keep people scared of you? Well, big man, I sure as hell ain't scared of you!"

He was silent for a long moment. "I ought to break you in two, Smoke. I ought to smash your smart mouth and teach you so's you'll never forget." He bit his lip and stared at me. "I've whaled you until my hand ached, but I can see now that it wasn't hard enough. I should have broken you, boy, years ago. Broken you so's you'd behave and not bring me grief and trouble now."

"Like you broke Luther, huh? Or worked on Ma until she believes you're some kind of a god?" I turned and opened the door as wide as it would go. "Go on, get out of here and leave me alone. You ain't nothing special, Cord. You've just got people fooled into believing you are."

He stepped to the door, but he turned and doubled up his fist. "Don't ever stand up against me, Smoke. I'll get what I want and I'll kill the man who stands in my way. Even you."

I watched him go down the stairs, a dead, uneasy feeling in my stomach. I hadn't meant to spill over like that but things seemed to pile up on me, like they did on Luther, and I too had to hit out at anything that was handy. But I must have hit something pretty solid because I'd never seen Cord rocked back like that. Quite by accident I'd gotten through to him, but in a way that made him dangerous angry. Angry enough to look upon me as a menace.

16

That night the Guthrie lawyer came in on the evening train and went into an immediate huddle with Cord. Marshal Ledbetter had already telegraphed the facts, as he knew them, to Oklahoma City, and word came in that they were sending a government prosecutor since we had no legal recourse in Ponca City stronger than a Justice of the Peace. A judge was going to arrive in a few days to hold court.

Late in the evening, Luther's attorney came around, a thin man, as straight standing as an undriven nail. He had a reedy voice and a liking for striped suits and flowers in the lapel. He questioned me at great length, but seemed relieved to get it over with. When I asked what he thought of Luther's chances, he just looked at me sourly and walked out.

I hadn't spoken to Edna since Luther had been arrested, figuring that she never wanted to clap eyes on me again. But she surprised me by coming to my hotel room. I invited her inside and closed the door, then waited for her to speak her piece. Only it wasn't what I had expected.

"I need help, Smoke."

"And you think I can help?" I shrugged. "Tell me how."

"You can go and talk to Luther. He asked to see you."

This was a surprise. "I didn't think he'd want to see me. If I'd have kept my mouth shut, he wouldn't be in this fix."

"You can't be sure of that," she said quickly. "Smoke, I believe he's innocent. Can't you believe it?"

"Then he ought to change his story. The one he's told is pretty thin."

"He hasn't any story to change," Edna said. "Please, Smoke, believe in him. Believe in him because if you don't, he'll hang for something he didn't do."

"You really sound convinced," I said.

"Smoke, I'm begging you. Help me. Help Luther."

There was no doubting the sincerity in her voice, whether stemming from her love or her desire to believe; I couldn't be sure which. But it was there. I picked up my hat. "If Ledbetter will let me see him, I'll do it."

"And listen to him, Smoke. Listen with your heart."

"All right, Edna. You want to wait here?"

"No," she said quickly. "Cord didn't want me to come here, but I had to know that someone was fighting for him."

There was a good deal about this woman that I

didn't understand, but I was learning fast. "You really love him, don't you?"

"Yes," she said. "Weaknesses and all, Smoke. I love him."

"But not when you first came here," I said. "Not when you married him."

She was not going to lie to me, or pretend; I could see that. "No, I didn't love him then, Smoke. I married him to get away from Chicago. Then I fell in love with him." She gave me a direct look as though daring me to find anything cheap in her. "Smoke, I wasn't always proud of myself. In a big city, with no one to care what happens to you, you have to make out the best you can."

"You had your aunt. . . ."

"She ran a saloon on the south side," Edna said. "I hustled beer and picked the pockets of the drunks."

I took a deep breath and let it out slowly. She had laid it out for me; I doubt if she could have made it plainer. Yet how could I judge her on what she had been? The Edna I knew was all right, honest and playing the game straight.

Before I closed the door, I said, "You want my opinion, I think Luther got himself a better woman than he bargained for."

Then I walked down the hall to the marshal's room. I had to give my name through the door before he would open it, and once inside he patted me to see if I was trying to sneak a pistol to Luther.

"I'll wait outside," he said pleasantly. "Half-hour all right?"

"Yes, and thanks."

The door closed and I drew up a chair by the bed. Luther propped himself up on one elbow; his wrist was handcuffed to the bed rail. "I'm getting damned tired of laying down," he said.

"You look well fed."

"Three meals a day and not a lick of work," he said. Then the humor drained away, leaving his worry exposed, like rocks at low tide. "Smoke, I've thought a lot about what you did, giving the marshal the rope. And I guess the reason you did is because you're honest. And right now I need an honest man on my side."

"Hell, Cord would . . ."

Luther waved his hands, silencing me. "I don't want to talk about Cord. It's you I want to make understand. Smoke, I didn't kill Wade Everett. That's a fact and no matter what anyone says, they can't change that. I know there's evidence against me, but it's only circumstantial. When Heck Overland swears on the witness stand that I left his place in the early evening after Cord and I had a beef, it will look bad, but it don't mean I went to Everett's place and killed him."

"What was the argument about, Luther?"

He laughed without humor. "The same old

thing, when I'm going to be permitted to think for myself. We didn't settle anything, Smoke. Who can settle anything with Cord when you can't even understand him? After I left Heck's place, I just rode along, free and easy, stopping when I felt like it, trying to figure a way out."

"A way out of what?"

He looked at me as though trying to figure out whether I was playing cagey or dumb. He must have thought the latter for he said, "A way out of the mess I'm making out of my life. Smoke, I love Edna. I'm glad I married her. She's my wife and I don't want another man doing for her, making her smile; not even my own brother. Cord picked her for me, like I was feeble-minded or something and couldn't choose for myself."

"You didn't have to take her."

"Didn't I?" Luther smiled. "Smoke, he never let up on me, always asking whether I'd written her, and what I wrote, and telling me what I should write. He was always talking about her, building a fester in a man's mind." Luther shook his head. "Cord knows how to work on a man, Smoke. You don't realize because you've always been so contrary. But I was never that way, which is why I'm in this mess right now."

"The lawyer Cord hired will prove that you didn't do it."

"Nonononono!" He seemed almost angry. "Smoke, he won't prove it because he isn't supposed to. Listen to me, Smoke. Everyone doubted me, even you. Yes you did, when you turned me in. Ma did and I guess still does because she cries when she comes here. And Cord, he thinks I'm guilty as hell. All he can talk about is the dirty tricks his lawyer will have to pull to get me off." He paused. "But there is only one person who believes without even asking. Edna."

"She loves you," I said simply.

"Is that so, Smoke? How do you know for sure?" His hand shook when he raised it to his face. "God, can't you see I've got to know?"

"She told me," I said. "Told me in a way that I could never doubt." I wondered then if Luther knew about Edna's life in Chicago, and decided that he didn't. "You've got a wife, Luther. One who'll stick by you."

He cried then. I went to the window and looked out until he gathered himself under control. Finally he said, "Thanks, Smoke. I'm all right now." I turned back to him. "She loves me, Smoke; I made her love me. Cord had nothing to do with this."

"That's right," I said. "Cord had nothing to do with it."

He fell silent for a time, then said, "Someone stole my rope and hung Wade Everett with it. Find out who, Smoke."

"I'll try."

"Watch Bill Hageman," Luther said. "He hasn't been in town since I was arrested."

"Maybe he's busy."

"Busy? Doing what? Everyone else comes and goes but Hageman stays home."

"You don't think . . ."

"He had reason enough, and chance enough!" Luther lay back on the bed. "Keep your eyes and ears open, Smoke. Sooner or later you'll find out who killed Everett, because I sure to God didn't."

Bud Ledbetter unlocked the door when I knocked and I went back to my room to consider the things Luther had talked about. He was telling the truth, like Edna told the truth. His story was straight-told and too mixed up to be a lie. You've heard good liars. Every little detail falls into place, all the reasons are there; that's because a liar has time to figure the story out. Luther didn't and the truth sounded pretty limp. All of which set me to thinking. To steal the rope and hang Everett, time had to be juggled, and stories warped to make them ring true.

Where does a man start to unravel something like this? I asked myself this and didn't know. Difficult as it was, I tried to think of Bill Hageman as a killer, but the role didn't wear well on him. Even if he broke the O'Dare hold across the river, he wasn't in a position to buy, and if he could steal it, he lacked the money to make anything out of it. Only the O'Dares could profit by Wade Everett's death, and then only by a small bit of land.

The prosecutor was certainly going to make a major issue of that.

I went back to Ledbetter's room and knocked.

"Who is it?"

"Smoke O'Dare, sir. Can I talk to you?"

The key grated in the lock, then Ledbetter stepped outside, locking the door immediately. "What's on your mind?"

"I want to know if you've checked on the others, like Bill Hageman?"

"Yes," Ledbetter said, smiling. "Smoke, I don't take anything for a fact without evidence. I even checked Cord, and you."

"What about the farmers?"

"Pretty difficult there," he said, "but I think they're all accounted for at the time the hanging took place. The bachelor, Higgins, was a little difficult to place, but Mooney and his family said that Higgins left their place around five. Higgins said he was going home to do the chores. I couldn't get anyone to swear to this, but the chores were all done when Vince Randolf stopped there two hours later." He shook his head. "I know how you feel, son, but you're fighting shadows now."

What avenues had I left unexplored? Perhaps Ledbetter had asked this of himself, for he said, "Smoke, these things just happen. The evidence against Luther is pretty final."

"I know that," I said and went back to my room.

17

There wasn't much sleep for me that night and the next day was a dragged-out affair that never seemed to end. The judge and the prosecutor arrived on the evening train and while the judge put up notices for the court, the prosecutor had a conference with Bud Ledbetter.

The next morning I shaved and put on a new suit since Ledbetter had already told me that I would be called as a witness. Since we had no regular courthouse, the Grange Hall had to serve. The judge's bench was set up, along with chairs and a table for the lawyers.

The hall was packed; everyone for twenty miles came in to witness the trial.

Ma didn't come in and I didn't blame her. It was difficult for me to sit there and listen to the prosecutor paint Luther black. He established a motive, pure and simple: Luther was a cattleman and just hated farmers. This motive was strengthened when Wade Everett's widow took the stand and described in vivid detail the brawl between Luther and her dead husband. A little crying here made a solid effect on the jury and then the prosecutor called me on the stand and made me swear that the testimony Mrs. Everett had given was the gospel truth.

I kept watching the judge, a grizzled man who listened with exactness to everything said. Watching him, I was kind of glad he was there because I didn't think an unprejudiced jury could be raised in Ponca City, and this man seemed to be the kind who would squash quickly any tendency to reach snap decisions when a man's life was at stake.

Heck Overland came in from Rindo's Springs to testify to the time Luther left his place. Heck was in a surly mood and tried to leave the impression that he was putting himself out by coming over, as though there were things to do in that blowed-away town of his.

The day ended with the prosecutor as happy as a chicken-fed weasel. The jury was remanded to a constable appointed by the court and locked up for the night. Ledbetter took Luther into tow and I went to my hotel room.

I spent a most miserable night and the next morning woke bleary-eyed and mad at the world. An early breakfast at the restaurant down the street failed to cheer me. While I was finishing my coffee, Vince Randolf came in and sat down at my table. I hadn't seen Vince since the day Ledbetter took away his shotgun.

"Do you mind, Smoke?"

"No," I said. "You're welcome to sit down."

Randolf didn't smile; the situation was too grave for that. "You're not a man to hold the foolishness of another man against him, are you, Smoke?"

"I guess you're not either," I said.

"We seem to understand each other," Randolf said. "Probably because we're men of peace. I'm ashamed to say that it's taken me this long to cool off and think straight, but now that I have, I'd like you to answer something personal."

"Why not? The O'Dares are an open book now."

"Didn't mean it that way," Vince Randolf said. "But we ought to look at a few facts. Let's say that Luther did hang Everett. If so, what was his reason?"

"The prosecutor made a good point there," I said.

Randolf waved it aside. "Smoke, he's talking about a maniac who kills because he hates. That don't fit your brother, not by a damn sight." He paused and stroked his chin. "Smoke, let's say that Luther killed Everett because Wade found out that Luther had been doing all the rustling." I opened my mouth to speak but Randolf held up his hand. "Let me finish my supposin's. If Luther's been rustling, then where's the money he got for the cattle? Hell, we all know that he never had two nickels to crack together in his jeans. Cord even paid for the wedding."

Funny how something like that will pop up and hit you right between the eyes. Randolf was right! Where was the money if Luther sold the cattle? It didn't fit at all, him always hollering all the time about being broke. And he was.

This was the killer's flaw, the uncoverable flaw!

"What I said makes a difference?" Randolf asked softly. "You got a look in your eyes, Smoke."

"Yeah, it makes a difference," I said.

"Figured I owed you something on account of some hard thoughts, Smoke." He got up then and went out.

I sat at the table, trying my best to fit this important piece into the rest of the puzzle. My first impulse was to find Cord, for lifetime habits are strong. But I checked that and decided to play this hand to a finish myself.

The prosecution completed its case in the early afternoon and now the Guthrie lawyer Cord had imported got up and began to move about the courtroom, his hands clasped behind him. He made a long-winded speech about justice until I began to grow impatient with the man. I wanted to get on the stand and tell what I knew but he was keeping me off with his fool speech.

Since Heck Overland had already been cross-examined he was not recalled to testify, and to my great surprise, I wasn't either. The defense lawyer, I realized, had no witnesses for Luther. All he could do was to call Edna to the chair and have her testify to Luther's sterling character. I doubted whether this did any good, for the jury sat stony-faced and the judge seemed a little bored.

Cord was finally summoned and sworn in. Bud Ledbetter was sitting two chairs over and I whispered to him, "Why didn't they call me?"

He shook his head. "Your testimony is too damaging to Luther's case." He held his finger before his lips and I sagged back, my opinion of court procedure pretty bleak. What I couldn't understand was why the word rustling never came into the court conversation; both attorneys seemed to avoid it as though there was a common agreement between them. And I thought it very important; the whole affair hinged on it.

"Will you state your name?" the defense lawyer was asking.

"Cord Adrian O'Dare."

"You're the defendant's older brother?"

"That's right," Cord said. He looked around the room, his glance touching Luther, who sat slouched in his chair. Because I had seen that look a dozen times a day I recognized it as Cord's "straighten up" look.

"Mr. O'Dare, were you aware that the defendant quarreled with the deceased prior to his death?"

"It was news to me," Cord said. "Luther'd been acting odd of late."

"What do you mean, odd?"

"Well, moody. Quick to fly off the handle."

Cord rubbed his face a moment. "But Luther wasn't a man who'd kill."

The prosecutor popped up like a released spring. "Your honor, that is a conclusion and should be stricken off the record!"

"So ordered," the judge said. "The counsel for defense will refrain from leading the witness. Ask only direct questions about events of which he has knowledge."

"No more questions," the lawyer said and whipped around, returning to his chair.

The prosecutor descended like a hawk after a rabbit. "Mr. O'Dare, you claim that the defendant is incapable of violence, yet that is hardly borne out by previous testimony, is it?"

"There's a difference between fighting and killing," Cord said. "Don't try and twist around what I say."

"I wouldn't think of it, sir." He jammed his hands in the armholes of his vest. "Mr. O'Dare, I take it that Wade Everett's death was a shock to you."

"It was."

"And what was your first thought, sir? Surely you bore no love for the man, yet you were shocked, or so you say."

"Your honor," the defense counsel said, rising, "I fail to see the point to this line of questioning."

"If I may indulge your patience," the prosecutor said, bowing, "I think I can make my point clear."

"I feel that the line of questioning is within

proper definition," the judge said. "You may proceed, Prosecutor."

"Thank you," he said, turning back to Cord. "Now, what was your thought when you learned that Wade Everett had been killed?"

"I don't remember," Cord said flatly.

"Ah, now isn't that strange? Your memory seems quite lucid on all other points. Wasn't your immediate thought that your brother had committed the crime and that you would have to cover for him?"

It seemed to me that everyone started shouting at once; Luther's lawyer was on his feet, demanding attention, and the judge was banging his gavel, trying to restore order.

Cord was boiling mad. He reared erect and shouted, "I won't answer any more of your goddamn, twisting, lying questions!" He stalked out of the courtroom then, in spite of the judge's warning, and it was the worst thing he could have done, for nearly every man there believed that Cord had only done so because the prosecutor had hit upon the truth.

Finally the judge got the court calmed down and Luther's lawyer called him to the stand. The room seemed cooler and there were unfriendly faces wherever I looked.

"Your name, please?" The defense attorney was asking the questions.

"Luther Lovelock O'Dare."

"Mr. O'Dare, will you tell the court in your own words your exact movements during the evening and night in question?"

There wasn't much to Luther's story when it was spoken out loud. Before that audience of very quiet people it sounded as thin as boarding-house molasses. And he didn't do a good job of telling it either, halting often, sweating a lot, and pausing to wipe his face. He was very nervous and once had to stop until he could control the shakes. In all, it seemed like he was guilty as hell and trying badly to lie his way out of it.

No one believed the story; at least I saw no visible sign of sympathy in the jury's faces. He told how he had left Overland's place, taking the Ponca City road. Then he had changed his mind, going straight home instead, only there was no one there. He ended up by swearing to God that he hadn't been near Wade Everett's place and had no idea how the rope got there.

The counsel for defense turned the whole thing over to the prosecutor, who looked like a chicken hawk as he stepped toward the witness chair.

"Mr. O'Dare, your story is touching, but let's end this farce and throw ourselves on the mercy of the court."

"Huh?" Luther said.

The lawyer was smiling like a horse thief. "Come, sir, you're an intelligent man. How can you sit there and deny the evidence?" He counted it on his fingers, particularly the unaccounted-for time after he left Overland's. Luther just sat there, head down, while the lawyer made a criminal of him. I wanted to shout to him, tell him to get his damned head up; but the habit was too strong in Luther, and Cord had pushed him down too many times in his life for me to expect him to rise up manlike now.

The prosecutor stepped back, waving his hands disgustedly. "Your honor, the defense has not produced one shred of evidence to support this man's claims. We have proven both motive and opportunity, along with establishing the rope as being the defendant's personal property. On this we rest our case."

Luther went back to his chair. The judge banged with his gavel. "The jury will retire to consider their verdict."

Each man in that roped-off section looked at each other, then Eli Sugerman, the shoemaker, got up and said, "Your honor, we don't want to waste anyone's time. We already made up our minds."

"I see. And what is your verdict?"

"Guilty as sin," Sugerman said, then sat down.

There wasn't a sound in that room until the judge spoke. "Court will be in recess until five o'clock, at which time I shall pass sentence."

18

The suddenness of the verdict stunned me more than the verdict itself; I could not conceive of men so casual as to toss over a man's life without lengthy deliberation. Ledbetter took charge of Luther, taking him back to the hotel while I went down the street and entered Pete Lanahan's place. The trial drew the crowd and the heat promoted the thirst, so Pete did a fine business, seeing as how this was the middle of the week.

I edged up to the bar and ordered a beer. Then I noticed Heck Overland standing on my left. He looked at me and said, "Didn't take 'em long to take his size, did it?"

"He didn't do it," I said.

"Takes a fool or a smart man to buck evidence," he said. He hoisted his beer, then wiped his mouth with the back of his hand.

Suddenly a full-bloom suspicion of this man loomed in my mind and I knew I was standing next to a liar. Don't ask me how. I suppose it's that a liar always has something glib to say, something just right; he can afford it since most everything he says is stretching the truth anyway.

Then too, I believed Randolf when he said that Luther was too broke to be crooked. A man rustled for money, no other reason. And Heck Overland had lied when he said that Luther had been shipping from Rindo's Springs. The man was a liar and I was suddenly very determined to prove it.

"Did you know Wade Everett?" I asked.

"Nope," Overland said blandly. "Perfect stranger to me." He looked at me. "I don't get over this way much. Got things of my own to do. Wouldn't be here now if it wasn't my civic duty."

A wind of caution blew softly and something began to tickle the back of my mind but I couldn't get it to stand still so I could examine it. Then I remembered and had a hard time keeping my face straight.

"You say you never knew Everett? Funny, because when I mentioned him at your place not so long ago you said right off that he was a farmer."

Overland frowned. "What's got into you, kid? You trying to make me out something or other?"

There was a span of difference in size between Heck Overland and me, but this was something I really wanted to buy into. So I said, "I was just wondering how much you say is the truth and how much is a lie."

It don't take much to bring quiet to a place; silence surely fell suddenly in Pete Lanahan's saloon. Overland looked at me steadily. "You're a little sawed-off to climb a big tree, sonny."

"I'll make it plainer," I said. "You're a liar twice, once when you said you never knew Wade Everett and the other when you told me that Luther'd shipped stock from your pens."

He would have to hit me for saying that; I knew it and was ready when he swung. My size made ducking easy; he was too big to be graceful. My beer stein made a lovely weapon and I shattered it across the crown of his head.

Heck stumbled against the bar and went down to one knee. I reached for his beer mug, knowing that I was going to need it, but I got careless and only succeeded in knocking it off the bar. I stepped back because Heck was getting to his feet.

From down the bar someone with an old grudge to settle and not enough nerve to do it alone, slid a full whiskey bottle toward me. I grabbed it as Overland charged. There was no ducking this time. His arms encircled my waist and he began to apply a strangling pressure. I had only one chance and took it, smashing the full bottle dead center on his forehead. The strength went out of him like water draining from a sink and he went to all fours, shaking his head from side to side. Broken glass sparkled in his hair and blood ran down his face.

I had expected that one to end the fight but when he didn't go flat, a new and sudden panic seized me. Run; every instinct shouted this, but a man has his pride and I waited for him to get up. Then I kicked him in the face, arching him backwards, and he fell flat.

He growled like a bear and rolled over, trying to get up again. I let him make it as far as his hands and knees, then gave a running jump, landing with both knees into his kidneys. You could have heard that yell for three blocks and I rolled away from him, coming to my feet on the other side, away from the bar.

Heck was hurt bad, but there was animal strength in the man. He moaned and pawed the sawdust-covered floor and flung handfuls of it away from him, like a bull ripping turf. The customers of Lanahan's were giving us both a lot of room; they made a solid circle around us. Running now, even if I wanted to, was impossible.

I never expected Heck Overland to get to his feet, but he did. He staggered about, nearly blind with pain, but still groping for me, cussing me in his deep voice. I couldn't just stand there; I had to close with him. Hitting him in the jaw was out of the question. I found that out after I brought one up from the floor and nearly smashed my hand. Overland rocked back on his heels, spat out a broken tooth, but didn't go down or even show signs of being hurt.

He swung furiously a few times at the air; I'd already danced back out of reach. I tried belting him in the stomach but that was like hitting the side of a freight car with your bare hands. Overland grunted and swung some more, and this time he was a lot luckier, or I was getting careless. The blow caught me on the side of the head, lifted me clean off my feet and sent me whipping across the sawdust with a vast, cavern-like roaring in my head. Getting to my own feet was a real chore, but it had to be done. Overland was coming my way, walking with short, solidly planted steps. His arms were searching about, trying to find me, and I stepped under them, driving my fist hard against his heart.

His mouth opened in a shrill cry, then he started to gag for wind. I hit him again, in the same spot, and once more he started to fall. Overland fell as only a two-hundred-and-twenty-pound man can fall, like tall timber, shaking every window in the place.

Pete Lanahan braced his arms on the bar, hoisted himself and looked over at Heck Overland stretched out on the sawdust. Then he looked at me and shook his head as though he couldn't believe it.

Had I so desired, I could have had a gay time on the free drinks everyone wanted to buy, but my main concern now was to get out and to find Cord as quick as I could. Excuses were hard to make, but I made them and left Lanahan's; they were still trying to get Heck Overland to stand on his own feet.

I checked at the hotel and the clerk said he

thought Cord was upstairs. I tried Ledbetter's room, but he wasn't there, or in mine. Then I went down the hall to ask Edna. When I knocked, her voice sounded a little startled.

"Who is it?"

"Me, Smoke. Have you seen Cord?"

For a moment I thought she wasn't going to answer me, then she opened the door. "Come in," she said, then I saw Cord standing by the window, watching the street.

I didn't pay any attention to Edna; Cord was the man I wanted to see. He looked at me, saw the bruise growing on the side of my face, and asked, "What have you been into?"

"I just called Heck Overland a liar and whipped the hell out of him."

Cord stared for a moment, then laughed. "You drunk?"

"Cold sober. Go over to Lanahan's and take a look at him."

He believed me then. He said, "What is this, Smoke? You going on the prod or something?"

"Luther didn't kill Wade Everett or rustle any stock," I said. "I was in Rindo's Springs the same day I found Luther's rope in Everett's barn. Heck said that Everett was a farmer, yet he claims to have never heard of the man before. He also said that Luther had been shipping stock and that you'd been covering for him. That's a lie because Luther was always broke. He didn't have a pot to p . . ." I managed to check that in time, then I noticed Edna was looking at Cord, not paying attention to me. "He never had any money, Cord, and no one rustles for the hell of it."

"What do you think you're proving?" Cord asked. "By God, if you know something, let's go see the judge."

"That's all I know," I said. "But it's enough to get Luther off, ain't it, Cord?"

"Sure it is," he said quietly. He put his hand on my shoulder and smiled the way he always smiled. "I've said some rough things to you, Smoke. Thought some bad things too. How can I ever take 'em all back?"

"Aw," I said. "You don't have anything to take back."

He nodded. "Go on back to your room. I'll go and see the judge and we'll put Overland back on the stand. We'll wring him like a chicken. Likely Overland's been rustling and using us as a blind."

Did you ever have an unbearable weight lifted from your mind? Cord lifted one from mine and I went back to the hotel room whistling. Edna had been crying when I left, but those were happy tears; I never like to be around a woman when she turns mushy.

In my own room I lay down for a while and tried to forget the headache Heck Overland's belt had given me. The bandage on my scalded arm needed changing but I was too lazy, and too pleased to get up and walk three blocks to the doctor's office. I wanted to sleep, and I did, the first untroubled rest I'd known since my all-night ride. Late in the afternoon, when it came time to go back to the courtroom, I felt refreshed and relieved, and very confident that the judge would reverse the jury's verdict.

The place was jam-packed as usual, and I took my place behind the defense counsel's table. The judge rapped for order and the room grew very quiet. He cleared his throat and said, "After careful and due deliberation of the evidence presented, and allowing for certain inconclusive elements, I am prepared to render a sentence. Will Luther O'Dare please rise and face the court."

Luther did; he looked squarely at the judge.

"This court, having found the defendant, Luther Lovelock O'Dare, guilty, now imposes the sentence of twenty years at hard labor in the federal penitentiary at Fort Smith, Arkansas."

The Grange Hall became a bedlam of sound and some of the people even cheered. Luther looked like a man stunned mortally; he would have fallen had not the defense attorney caught him. Edna, who sat a few seats to the right, wailed once and clapped both hands over her face. I looked for Cord. He sat stone-still, his face absolutely expressionless.

Bud Ledbetter took charge of Luther then and

took him directly to the depot, locking him in the express room. I suppose he figured the hotel was no longer a safe place; Cord and I might try to break him out.

Battering my way through the milling crowd, I grabbed Cord by the coat. "What the hell went wrong? Wouldn't the judge listen? Cord, talk to me!"

"Not now," Cord said, shoving my hands away. "Leave me alone, Smoke."

He got up and shoved and pushed until he was outside. The defense attorney was stuffing papers into his briefcase when I sided him. "A lot of good you did for him," I said.

"There wasn't much to work with," he said. Then he looked at me and added, "You made a tight case for the prosecution."

Edna remained in her chair, crying. I took her out of there and back to her hotel room. She lay on the bed and buried her face in the pillow, her shoulders shaking. By rights I suppose I ought to have left her alone, but the truth was, I needed company myself pretty bad.

"I was so sure the judge would let him off," I said. "What went wrong, Edna?"

She turned and looked at me. Tears made a slick smear on her cheeks and her eyes were red-rimmed. "Wrong? The whole rotten thing is wrong! Is God punishing me for loving a decent man? Oh, Luther, Luther, what have I brought on you?" She fell back on the bed, crying anew.

This made very little sense to me, so I waited until the crying died out to a few sniffles. "What's the matter with you, Edna? Or is there something the matter with us?"

She shook her head from side to side, violently. "I don't care about you or Ma or anyone but Luther. Stop them, Smoke! Don't let him be taken from me!"

"Hell . . ." I began, then closed my mouth. What did she expect me to do? Back East they'd have thrown the case out of court for lack of evidence, but this was Oklahoma, where justice was rough and sudden and damned final; Luther was lucky he wasn't hung.

19

A crying woman is not my idea of a conversationalist so I left Edna alone. I stayed in my own room for a while but found the loneliness unbearable. The traffic on the main drag had thinned astonishingly; the farmers had all gone home and the boardwalk idlers had dwindled to a dribble of townsfolk who never did much but stand around anyway.

From the east end of the street I saw Ma's buggy approaching. Bill Hageman was driving and Julie was sitting in the back seat. My first thought was to get out of sight so Ma wouldn't see me, but then I couldn't hide the rest of my life. While Hageman tooled the rig to the hotel, I went down the stairs, arriving on the porch as he dismounted to tie up.

He said, "Lige Binghan stopped off with the verdict. Where's Luther being held?"

"At the express office. Train's due in an hour or so."

I stepped under the hitch rail to help Ma down but Bill shook his head. "Better let me, Smoke."

He was right. Ma would likely hit me if I got that close to her. Judging from her eyes, all puffed and red, she'd been doing more than her share of crying. She seemed so much older now and I felt guilty because I was responsible.

Julie came to the sidewalk to stand. She didn't say anything, just touched my hand then squeezed it gently. From across the street Cord emerged from Lanahan's, saw Ma and ran over, his arms outstretched. Ma wailed and hugged him and said, "My boy, my dearest boy, going to prison!"

"Now, Ma," Cord said, patting her shoulders. "Let's stay steady now."

"You're so strong, Cord. So much of a comfort." Her hand came up and brushed at the dangling lock of hair. "I'd die without you, son. I'd just up and die."

"Don't talk like that, Ma. Please don't." His glance swung to me as though this was my fault too.

"If you want to see Luther," Bill said, "you'd best get on to the depot. There isn't much time."

"I just couldn't," Ma said, her eyes tear-filled. "Seeing him with his hands locked together, I just couldn't." For a moment her crying was uncontrollable, then she took a renewed grip on her emotions. "I'm an old woman; I'd be seeing him for the last time."

"You should go, Ma," Cord said. "You'd be a comfort to him."

"If you think that's best," she said. "You always know best, Cord."

He put his arm around her and they walked slowly down the street. The sun was down now and deep shadows built beneath the building overhangs. A few lamps were lighted and by the time we reached the other end of the street, Ponca City had settled down for the night.

The depot sat alone, a hundred yards beyond the street. When I stopped, Bill looked at Julie, then me. "I think I'll get a drink. A stiff one."

He retraced his steps toward Lanahan's. Julie asked, "Aren't you going on to the depot, Smoke?"

"No," I said. "I couldn't face Luther now, having failed him."

"You did what you thought was right," she said. "Smoke, you can't spend the rest of your life blaming yourself."

"But he's innocent!" I was angry, unreasonably so. Particularly at the judge who wouldn't listen to something that made sense. "I've changed my mind. I'm going to the depot, but not to see Luther."

I left her standing there and trotted toward the main railroad building. I knew that the judge had already checked out of the hotel, so I figured he'd be waiting to take the train. Normally, only a few loafers hung around the depot, but that night the stationmaster had quite a crowd. Luther was being held in the express room and Ma and Cord were in there, saying good-bye. The two attorneys stood on the platform with their bowlers and twenty-five-cent cigars, exchanging pleasantries or comparing notes; which, I didn't know or care.

The judge was sitting inside, briefcase at his feet. I went in, seeing that he was alone. He looked at me sharply. "What is it, young man?"

"I want to talk to you," I said.

"My time is short, but if you can make it brief . . ."

"I'll make it brief," I promised. "It beats me how you can sit there and pass out twenty years of hard labor to a man after you've heard evidence that proves one of the witnesses was a liar."

"I beg your pardon." He acted real insulted.

"Yeah, you do that, Judge. Hell, Overland was lying his head off when he said he didn't know Everett. He knew Everett all right, and he lied when he said that Luther ever shipped stolen cattle from Rindo's Springs."

The judge's attention picked up considerable at that and his eyes became as sharp as drill points. "What's this you're saying?"

"You know what I'm saying. How many times does a thing have to be repeated before you understand it?"

The train whistled for the grade crossing a few miles out and the judge stood up, briefcase under his arm. "Young man, you're raving. Now if you'll excuse me, I believe that's my train coming."

I shouldn't have done it, but I grabbed his arm and swung him around so hard that he sat back down. "To hell with your train! You hear me out or you ain't going to get on it."

"I'm afraid I may have to call Marshal Ledbetter here," he said.

"Call him then, because I want him to hear it too."

"You're serious," the judge said, sort of surprised. "Believe me, young man, what you're saying is strange to me."

For a moment I thought he was lying, then I knew that he wasn't. "Didn't my brother, Cord, talk to you?"

"I allow no one to speak to me after a jury returns a verdict; I have no intention of being intimidated or influenced while I'm pondering a decision."

"But he tried to see you?"

"I doubt that very much," he said. The train was slowing down and the judge got up again, moving toward the door. I followed him while trying to figure a way to stop him without landing in jail.

"Judge, won't you wait? Won't you please listen?"

He turned to me, his voice gentle and very kind. "Young man, I can understand your feelings, and believe me, I'm in sympathy with you. Had the evidence been anything but strongly circumstantial, I most certainly would have sentenced your brother to hang. As it is, there was strong doubt, a lack of conclusive proof. If in the future any facts present themselves that warrant reopening the case, rest assured that your brother's sentence can be set aside."

The train came in, blowing and snorting, and the judge walked away with hurried strides. I stood against the dark side of the depot and watched him board. I thought, there goes Luther's last chance.

From the baggage room, Marshal Bud Ledbetter emerged, his left hand handcuffed to Luther's right. Ma and Cord were there and Ma was nearly wild with grief. The marshal hustled Luther onto the train and then the brakeman waved his lantern.

I stood there while it pulled away, leaving behind a fog of gritty cinders and the stink of hot machinery. Cord and Ma were walking toward me and Cord had his arm around Ma while she cried. I could see that they intended to pass me by, so I said, "Wait a minute, Cord."

My voice must have shocked them for they both stopped quickly and stared at the shadows. Then I stepped out where they could see me.

"Smoke," Cord said, "will you just go away?"

"Not yet," I said. "You didn't talk to the judge, Cord. You didn't tell him anything."

He didn't try to lie out of it; that's one thing I

have to give him credit for. "No," he said, "I didn't. I thought it over, Smoke, and then I knew it wouldn't do any good. All we would have proved was that Heck Overland lied a little. Luther would still have been as bad off as he is now."

Ma raised her head and looked at me. "What are you trying to do, put your guilt on my son?" Her arms tightened about Cord. "Shame on you, Smoke. Oh, you're a terrible boy! The devil's in you!"

"Come on, Ma," Cord said. "I'll get you a room at the hotel." He started to move on, then spoke to me again. "Why don't you just saddle your horse and get the hell out of the country?"

I didn't answer him because that sounded like good advice. I waited until they disappeared on past the depot, then eased uptown to Pete Lanahan's. He was washing the beer taps with soda water and Bill Hageman was alone at a corner table. I crossed over and sat down.

Bill looked at me momentarily, then said, "I don't have to ask whether it was tough or not."

"Nothing will ever be any tougher," I said.

He shrugged. "A man never knows, Smoke."

I told him what I'd found out about Heck Overland. Bill listened carefully, then said, "Pete told me that you'd wiped the floor with Heck. A little hard to believe at first, but he convinced me." He paused to sip his beer. "If you're right, then that means that Luther's going to do some time that he don't have coming. And the rustler is laughing up his sleeve." His eyes met mine, steady-calm. "I could be that man, Smoke."

"I don't think you are," I said.

"No, I'm not. But Heck Overland could be."

"That's occurred to me," I said. "I know for sure the steers were shipped from there." I shook my head. "When it comes to having brass, Overland's got it, shipping stolen stock right under our noses."

"I don't know," Bill said. "Not many people get up to Rindo's Springs any more. Myself, I haven't been there for some time." He looked at me. "Overland left town right after the fight, I hear tell." He finished his beer, then pushed the glass aside. "You feel up to a little ride, Smoke?"

"Rindo's Springs?"

"I was thinking about how I've neglected the place," Bill said. "Downright unfriendly of me, ain't it? You got a gun?"

"At home," I said. "You bring yours along?"

"Yes," he said. "Seemed like only a hunch at the time, but now I'm glad I did. It's under the front seat of the buggy."

We got up and Bill put his beer stein on the bar. To Lanahan, he said, "Pete, you got a gun around here?"

"Yeah," Lanahan said. "Figurin' to shoot some-body?"

"No," Bill said. "Just wondered if I could borrow it."

"I guess," Lanahan said and dug around beneath the bar. He came up with a long-barreled Colt .45 and shoved it toward Bill, who rocked open the loading gate, checked the loads, then passed it on to me.

"You'll get this back," I said and Bill and I went out.

20

Since Bill Hageman had driven to town in the buggy, I went to the stable to rent a horse for him. When I came back, leading my own and the livery pony, Bill was standing on Lanahan's porch. He was wearing his gun.

In all the years I'd known him, I'd never seen him packing his six-shooter, but I must say that he wore it pretty casually, as though he had a long-standing familiarity with it. Me? I stuffed Pete Lanahan's .45 in my belt and let it go at that. Even when I practiced regular, I never could draw fast. But I knew which end did the damage and could point it fair to middling, which was about all the average westerner could do.

I had a notion to stop and tell Cord where I was going, in case Heck Overland did me in, but Bill was in a hurry to leave, so I let the idea slide by. We drifted out of town, not attracting any attention, and after thinking about it, I doubted that anyone saw us at all. Folks were in their homes now that the excitement was over.

Bill Hageman was never a man long on talk and our ride was one of silence. We stopped twice, once at a small creek, and another time at the edge of Rindo's Springs.

The place looked like a graveyard at night, absolutely dead. The wind husked dust along the main street, sculpturing the windrows it had already piled along the decaying boardwalk. A loose board banged on the old opera house roof, then the wind whined off to the hilly country beyond.

"Let's go have a closer look," I suggested.

"On foot," Bill Hageman said and dismounted.

That looked like a far walk to me, nearly three hundred yards, but since Bill was running things, I stepped from the saddle. We led our horses off the trail and tied them in a clump of bushes. With Bill leading, we soft-footed around the edge of town and threaded our way through a littered alley. Once I fell over a stack of old boxes and raised a clatter. Bill picked me up and said, "Why don't you just yell out and let Overland know we're coming?"

He started to move on, then stopped bolt-still when three shots hammered the night, the echo bucketing over the empty town. Bill didn't have to say a thing; when he started to run, I followed him.

Overland's String of Pearls was in the middle of the block, on our side, and three barked shins later we were both fighting to see who could get through the back door at the same time. Out front someone raced off the porch and mounted his horse. Closely following was the sound of a horse running down the street.

Bill cursed the darkness and the unfamiliar rooms, trying two doors before he found the one leading into the saloon. We ran through, kicking tables and chairs out of our way, but by the time we made the street, all that was left of the rider was a cloud of dust.

"Let's find Overland," Bill suggested.

I fumbled around until I found a kerosene lamp, then scratched a match. A man hardly realizes what a comfort a light is in a dark place until he has one in his hand. Since Bill was carrying his pistol unholstered, I decided I'd better play it smart and do the same. He took the lamp from me and began to move around the room, looking in all the dark spots.

We searched the back rooms, the ones we had stumbled through, but found no sign of Heck Overland. Then I remembered something. "He lives upstairs, Bill."

We went into the alley again, but the outside stairs were too rotten to trust. "Around the front," Bill said. "Our shy friend came from there."

After passing through the saloon again, we walked to the first gap between the buildings. Bill shined the lamplight into the crack and we saw the stairs. He went up first, two at a time, and found the top door open. I crowded in behind him, then wished that I hadn't.

Heck Overland was there all right, but he wasn't going to do us any good. He lay on his bed, leaking blood. His eyes were wide-staring as though he found the dark ceiling utterly fascinating. Right in the middle of his chest three slugs had been planted close enough to be covered with the palm of the hand.

I doubt that Overland ever knew what had hit him; he must have been asleep when the killer cut loose.

Bill Hageman cuffed the back of his hand against his hat brim, shoving it to the back of his head. "Someone sure knew his way around." He motioned toward the bed. "Without the light, a man would never know the bed was there."

"Let's get out of here," I suggested, suddenly discovering that a man is never as brave as he thinks he is.

"We ought to bury him," Bill said.

"All right. Can you get him down alone? I'll see if I can scare up a couple of shovels."

Digging a hole, then covering it up takes time; we buried Heck Overland in the alley. The night was pleasantly cool but we were both sweating by the time we were finished.

I leaned on my shovel and said, "You know, killing Heck was pretty stupid."

"Huh?" Bill gave the mound of earth a final pat, then pitched his shovel into a pile of rubble. "How's that, Smoke?"

"Well, Luther's been convicted of killin' Everett, and everyone will figure that whoever done that

240

has been rustling too. Seems to me that with Heck dead, folks will start to wondering if the wrong man wasn't sent to jail."

"What folks?" Bill asked.

"Well, hell, the people around Ponca City!"

"I don't think many of them ever come over here," Bill said. "Heck could have laid up there, dead for weeks, maybe a month before anyone ever found him. Then what was to say Heck wasn't shot and robbed?" He shook his head. "We're right back where we started, Smoke."

"You got any ideas?" I asked.

For a moment Bill said nothing, then, "Nope, but we'll flush him yet."

Right then I wouldn't have given a lead nickel for our chances. Fifteen minutes sooner and we'd have caught our man coming down those stairs, but then I guess a lot of good things are missed by fifteen minutes.

"Nothing more to do here," I said and Bill agreed. We walked out of the dead town to where our horses were tied. After we mounted I sat there and looked at Rindo's Springs and watched the wind eat away at it.

"Let's go, Smoke," Bill said and we started back to Ponca City.

21

A man can do a lot of thinking while he's riding and come up with some very odd answers. Maybe Bill was doing the same, but if he was, he was waiting for me to draw the first conclusions, which didn't take long for I've never learned to keep my mouth shut.

"Overland was killed to shut him up," I said. "Somebody's scared."

"That's no lie, but who?"

I didn't know but I intended to find out. "It was no secret what me and Heck fought about in Lanahan's," I said. "Any damn fool could have figured it out from our conversation before the fur flew."

"That's a big help," Bill said dryly. "I wonder where Randolf is tonight?"

"You don't think . . ." Then I laughed. "Naaaa! Not Vince."

Bill turned his head and looked at me. "Smoke, you can't tell everything about a man from his face. People ain't always what they seem."

I wondered if he was talking about Cord. That might sound strange, my willingness to include Cord in with everyone else as a suspect, but since I'd been suspicious of one brother, it wasn't hard for me to move on to the other. Anyway, I was sure going to ask Cord what he had been doing all evening. And I was going to get an answer. I guess Pete Lanahan's .45 made me feel man-sized.

When we got back to Ponca City, Bill took the horses to the livery stable while I went on to the hotel. The clerk was sleeping with a newspaper over his face and I cat-footed up the stairs without waking him. The upper hall was as dim as sin, the hotel owner being so stingy he'd only light one lamp at each end. I had no idea which room Cord had, but I was sure Edna would know; she'd just have to forgive me for waking her at three in the morning.

As I approached her door I stopped, for she was talking, not so loud I could hear her words, but talking nevertheless. Then I heard Cord's voice, indistinct, but still his, unmistakably. They sounded like they were arguing, then the voices cut off quick and I heard Edna step to the door.

There was no place to hide, just bare walls and a dozen doors. Quickly I backed, tried the first knob my hand reached and felt it give. I just managed to close it to an inch crack when Edna flung her door open.

"Just get out," she said flatly. "Cord, I would never help you, not after what you did to Luther. That was a cruel thing, and if I disappointed you, I'm glad."

Cord stepped out, his face darkly angry. "You can't change what you are, Edna. You're a tramp and it'll come out in time." He canted his head sideways and spoke more softly. "You know what Ma would do if she found out? She'd kick you off the place."

"Then go tell her," Edna snapped. "Tell her now. You've nothing to gain by keeping it from her."

Cord's shoulders rose and fell slightly. "Plenty of time, Edna. You remember what I told you now." He turned then and walked on down the hall.

Behind me bed springs squeaked unexpectedly and I nearly had my heart jump out of my throat. Ma's voice said, "Who's there?"

I was in her room!

Edna had closed her door and I guessed that Cord had started down the steps, so I quickly stepped out. Ma sat up in bed and yelled, "You stop there!"

The noise boomed through the silent building; probably my fear magnified it to those proportions. I crossed the hall in one leap and flung open Edna's door. She was getting into bed and quickly grabbed up her robe.

"Smoke! What are you doing here?"

Ma came out and crossed to Edna's door and began to hammer on it with her hand. "Edna, are you all right?"

"Answer her," I said in a flat whisper.

"I—I'm all right. Is there something wrong?"

"There was a man in my room," Ma said loudly. "A man!"

From down the hall a sleepy voice yelled, "Shut up and go to sleep!"

Another said, "Lady, at your age you should be so lucky!"

"I'm afraid," Ma said. "Let me in."

"Go back to bed," Edna implored. "Everything's all right, Ma."

"I'll go after I see for myself," Ma said firmly.

I recognized the metallic tone, and said, "Go ahead, open it."

When Edna opened the door, Ma stepped quickly inside. She started to speak, then saw me standing in the shadows.

"What are you doing in this room?" she asked.

"I wanted to talk to Edna," I said.

"Well, it can wait until morning," Ma said. "Run along now. It ain't proper that you should be in here with the door closed."

At any other time I would never have defied her, but this was winner take all and I'd been the disappointed loser too often. "I said I wanted to talk to Edna, Ma. Now you go back to bed and stop buttin' in my business."

Edna looked slightly alarmed. Ma gasped. "Why, how dare you talk to me like that? I'll tell Cord in the morning and he'll teach you some respect, he surely will."

"Well, you do that, Ma," I said. "But for now you can go to bed."

Her lip started to quiver, then she clasped her hands together and her expression turned somewhat saintly, and much put upon. "If that's the thanks I get for trying to raise you proper, then I wash my hands of you."

She slammed the door hard on her way out. Edna said, "Smoke, shame on you for . . ."

I held up my hand and she stopped talking. The door opened again and Ma stepped back inside, her curiosity having overpowered her.

"I'm your mother," she said. "What concerns Edna, concerns me."

"What was it you wanted to ask me, Smoke?"

"What did Cord want?"

"Cord?" Ma said. "Cord's in his room asleep."

"He was here, Ma," I said. She sniffed as though she didn't want to believe it, but was too polite to call anyone a liar.

"Well," she said, "suppose he was. My Cord has reasons for doing what he does. I've never seen fit to question them. Like his father, he's a headstrong man. Takes what he wants. If he was here, then everything's all right and a body hadn't ought to question it."

"And I say it ain't all right," I insisted. "What did Cord want, Edna?"

She bit her lip and looked from Ma to me, then back to Ma. "He wanted to know if I was going back to the home place in the morning."

"There," Ma said triumphantly. "You see? What were you trying to do, Smoke? Make Cord out wrong? A man who's never done a wrong in his life?"

I didn't pay any attention to her prattle; the truth had to come out and I was going to see what it looked like. "That ain't what Cord wanted," I said. "Cord threatened you, Edna. Why?"

"What lies!" Ma said, but Edna raised her hand and silenced her.

"Smoke," she said, "do you know where Cord was tonight?"

A sick feeling settled in my stomach. "I can make a good guess, Edna."

"It must have been something bad, because he wanted me to swear he'd spent the night—here."

Ma looked at Edna, her eyes round and pained. "Edna, what are you saying? Why are you telling those lies about Cord?"

"It's no lie, Ma," I said. "Cord killed a man tonight."

"No! You're both lying to me!" She almost pleaded. "My Cord wouldn't do a thing like that." Her fat hands fluttered and she appeared on the verge of tears. "He was such a good baby; he never cried. And I'd sing to him and he'd laugh. No, you're against him, Smoke. You've always been against him because he's strong and hand-some like his father. You're against him because he's a man and you're both just little people."

"He's evil," Edna said. "It's the truth, Ma. Smoke knows now, don't you, Smoke?"

"I know," I said.

Ma shook her head violently. "Oh, what terrible things to say! What monstrous lies! You only say that because you love Luther and want to hurt somebody, Edna. That Luther, he never could stand up to Cord like a man. Always moping around. And since he went bad you both want to make it Cord's fault."

"A man was killed tonight, Ma," I said, trying to make her understand. "How can you explain that away, Ma?"

She groped, tragically, blindly, and I stood there, tearing her world to pieces, board by board, scattering the wreckage about her. "He must have been protecting Luther. That's it! He always thought of everyone before he thought of himself. Look at the things he bought me. Pretty things. The dress. And the music box." She looked at me and shook her head as though I were too wicked to punish. "God will reach down and strike you for this, Smoke. He will. He'll punish you for saying things like that about Cord."

I had to give up; the truth was, I wanted to.

"Will you take her back to her room, Edna?"

She put her arm around Ma and led her out, and through the open doors I could hear Ma, talking, denying, disbelieving the things thrust at her so cruelly. Edna came back a moment later and closed the door. To me, she said, "Did you really have to do that, Smoke? The dreams were all she had."

"Ma's got to see what he really is," I said.

"I wonder if she ever will." She sat down on the edge of the bed. "He fooled me, Smoke, just like he's fooled everybody." She laughed without humor. "Once he told me he had a brother that wanted to get married. I thought he was joking. Who would want me, Smoke? What decent man?" She wrung her hands together. "I married Luther because I wanted to change."

"You have," I said. "Edna, believe that."

"Perhaps I do," she said. "But I've been hurt, Smoke. Can you understand why Cord pushed Luther into marrying me? Not because he wanted to make him happy, or me happy. No, it was only a cruel joke and Cord could laugh to himself every time he looked at us together."

This was, I decided, as close to the truth as a body could get, and wondered why I hadn't seen it before. Yet I could see the flaw that must have made Cord very angry. He had counted on Edna's cheapness showing through, counted on Luther's crushing disappointment, yet this had never happened. There was more to Edna than he had bargained for and they had fallen in love. How Cord must have hated that, for Luther to find happiness out of what was intended to be a cruel joke.

Surprisingly enough, I long suspected the scorn Cord had for Luther, who never walked quite as straight as a man should walk. And I suppose, in Cord's mind, he had brought about justice, wedding cheapness with weakness.

Edna spoke, breaking off my thoughts. "Smoke, did Cord kill that man, the one they accused Luther of killing?"

"I think so, Edna."

"Then he just stood there while Luther went to prison." She looked at me. "Smoke, could he really hate Luther that much?"

"I don't know," I said; I really didn't know.

"If I'd suspected," she said calmly, "I think I would have killed him."

There didn't seem to be much to talk about so I stepped to the door. Edna looked at me. "What are you going to do now, Smoke?"

I showed her the gun under my coat. "I'm going to face Cord and have it out. And if I have to, I'll shoot him."

She half raised from the bed and I stepped out into the hall, closing the door before she could reach it. I ran for the head of the stairs and took them two at a time. Bill Hageman was

250

sitting in the lobby and he stood up as I barged through.

"Whoa there," he said. "If there's a fire, I can carry a bucket as well as the next man."

"Cord was the man at Overland's," I said. A man has something to say, then he ought to come right out with it, even when it hurts.

"Well," Hageman said softly. "I didn't want to say that but it was my suspicion all the time. Seems that I know Cord better than you do, Smoke. Maybe it's because I'm older, or something. Cord's a grasping man, Smoke. And he's dangerous. You know that already."

"I'm going to send a telegram to Bud Ledbetter," I said. "They'll stop the train and bring Luther back."

"Better let me send it," he said. "Carry a little more weight that way, me not being in the family." He picked up his hat and walked out. I let him get three paces ahead, then decided to tag along.

The telegrapher was asleep and resented the rude awakening. He grumbled but gave us a blank and a pencil and Bill wrote out his message. The telegrapher read it, gave us both a startled look, especially me, then sent it over the wire. I paid for it, thirty-five cents, then we started back toward the center of town.

"What do you mean to do, Smoke? Wait for Ledbetter?"

"No," I said. "This is O'Dare business."

Bill walked in silence for a few paces. "Now you're thinking like Cord. One-man law."

"What do you want me to do, Bill? Give him a chance to sneak out of this?"

"I doubt he'll be able to do that," Bill said. We moved along toward the hotel. The street was dark and quiet, but in Lanahan's a few lamps still burned. Bill Hageman peeked over the lower stained-glass windows, then said, "He's in there, Smoke."

"Waiting," I said. "Bill, what should I do?"

"Do what he's doing, wait. Only we'll wait for Ledbetter." He turned toward Lanahan's door, then swung back, putting a hand on my shoulder. "I want you to stay out of any trouble that might come up, Smoke. He's still your brother."

He didn't have to remind me of that; I'd never forget it.

22

I wanted to go in first but Bill Hageman pushed me aside. Cord was sitting at one of the tables, a half-empty beer stein before him. He looked up, saw us, then said, "Lanahan left the place to me. Free beer."

"That sounds all right," Bill said, sitting down across from Cord. "You want to pull a couple, Smoke?"

I went behind the bar and filled two steins, taking them back to the table. Bill Hageman sipped his and I had to admire his composure. "A bad day today, huh, Cord?"

Cord nodded and managed to look a little downcast. The act made me wonder how much of this man's emotion was real and how much was an act. Or was it all act? At that moment he was nearly a stranger to me, an alien person with alien thoughts and feelings. The years of brotherhood seemed to melt away, leaving me with nothing save emptiness; I felt as though every bit of love I had offered him had been dirtied by his inability to understand it. I had been cheated. Had it been money, how easily I could have forgiven him. I would have pardoned him for stealing my woman, yes, even Julie. But a man's love for another is a sacred thing, born among the tenderest of emotions and offered sincerely.

"I thought you'd gone on home tonight," Bill said. "Didn't see you around town."

"I stayed in my room," Cord said. "You know how it is, Bill. I didn't want to talk to anyone."

"That's funny," Bill Hageman said softly. "I looked all over for you. Thought you'd like a game of cards."

I looked at Bill, realizing then that he had tricked me; he had no intention of waiting for Bud Ledbetter. He was going to try and take Cord himself!

Maybe I could help him by jarring Cord off balance. I said, "I just talked to Edna. She hadn't seen you either."

Cord looked at me blankly, but I noticed, very carefully.

"What's that supposed to mean?"

"Nothing," I said. "I just thought that maybe you went to Edna's room and didn't come out until a little while ago."

He put his hands flat on the table and managed to look downright insulted. "I ought to slap your dirty mouth shut," he said.

"Or maybe," Bill Hageman said, "you just wanted us to think you were in town when all the time you were over to Heck Overland's place putting three bullets in his chest." Bill smiled a little; I wondered where he got the nerve. "You see, Smoke and I only missed you by a few minutes. You was runnin' out the front door while we was stumblin' around in the back. But we buried Heck good and proper."

Never in my life had I seen Cord's face so colorless, or his expression so tight. He looked at Bill Hageman and then at me. "Just what is it you two pure people intend to do?"

"See that you don't go anywhere until Ledbetter gets back," I said. "We sent a telegram telling him that he's got the wrong man." While I spoke, I wondered from what well my calmness poured; I seemed to have no feeling of emotion. None at all. I suppose this was a reflection of Cord, a man without compassion, or love.

Cord said, "You two are too nosey for your own good."

"You rustled my cattle," Bill said flatly.

"Am I denying it?" Cord's voice was soft. "And others too. Those ranchers south of here have been blaming it on the Indians." He leaned slightly forward. "The trouble with you, Bill, is that you're shiftless. Without ambition you'll never amount to a damned thing."

"You think you'll ever amount to anything?" Bill asked.

"I'm the biggest man you'll ever see," Cord said. He glanced at each of us. "Look at yourselves, sitting there scared to death."

"I'm not denying I'm scared," Bill said. "I'm

scared when I find a rattlesnake in my blankets too." He straightened and dropped his right hand to his lap. "Cord, if you leave this room, then you'll have to leave two more dead men behind."

"That might not be hard to do," Cord said. He looked at me. "I told you once about never crossing me, Smoke. You wouldn't listen."

"For the first time," I said, "I'm just finding out how little you've had to say. But this still isn't easy for me."

"I guess it ain't," Cord said. "You always was sentimental as hell about things. Worse than Ma."

"Was Overland putting the squeeze on you?" Bill asked.

I looked at Cord and knew that Bill had the answer. "You never liked to have anyone push you, did you, Cord? What did Heck want? A little of the money? Wasn't his cut big enough?"

"Heck liked to talk," Cord said. "And he could say the wrong things. That made me nervous." He pushed his stein toward me. "You want to draw me a fresh beer, Smoke?"

"Draw your own," I said.

He laughed and got up, going behind the bar; I realized then what a position my foolish pride had put Bill and me into. Behind the bar, with his hands out of sight, Cord was in an ideal spot in case he wanted to shoot two people. He must have guessed what was going on in my mind, for he laughed. "Got you two boxed good, ain't I?"

Then because he was Cord O'Dare and proud and full of confidence, he came back to the table and sat down, placing the odds even again. "Overland made a mistake." His glance touched me. "And you made a bigger one by talking to the judge. The bastard might come back, figuring that if Heck lied once, then he might still be lying." He shook his head. "You see, I wasn't there the night Wade Everett was hung. I left right after Luther did." He paused, his brows wrinkled. "Heck said he'd talk unless he got some money. He got lead instead and I could have got away with it. Hell, it would have been weeks before anyone found him."

"But it wasn't weeks," Bill Hageman reminded him.

"You're right there," Cord said. His eyes played back and forth from Bill to me. Then he held up his fingers less than an inch apart. "I came that close to getting away with it, didn't I?"

"That's enough to hang you," Bill said.

I kept watching Cord, still trying to understand him. "You let Luther take the blame. You never lifted a finger to help him."

"Oh, that's not so," Cord said. "I hired a lawyer for him, the stupidest damn fool in Guthrie. What the hell is Luther anyway? A leaner. You move away from him and he falls down, then cries until you pick him up."

"Maybe it's because you never gave him a

chance to stand up," I said. "Or is it because you molded him into a weak-spined nothing just to see if you could do it?"

"I enjoyed it," Cord said. "It was like making something with my hands."

"You hate us, don't you, Cord? Me, Ma, all of us."

The pretended gaiety fled from his expression and his eyes turned slate-hard. "Hate you? No. How can you hate miserable, leaning, crawling bloodsuckers?"

"That includes Ma," I said.

"No," he said. "I love Ma. She's got faith, Smoke. Faith like a dog, the kind that never dies. A man needs that in a woman, but I've never found it in any other."

"Then you'd better take a look toward the hotel," I said. "Because over there is a woman who's lost that faith, Cord. Ma knows what you are. Maybe she won't admit it now, even to herself, but she sees the rottenness."

He hit me then, knocking me clean out of the chair. I skidded on the sawdust-covered floor and banged into the legs of a table, breaking one off and bringing the whole thing down on top of me. A loud bell started tolling in my head, but this faded, leaving only an ache in my jaw.

Bill Hageman was sitting stiffly. I said, "Now we know him like Overland did, and you know what Cord had to do to him."

I rolled clear of the table, hoping to distract Cord so Bill could draw. I may have succeeded, but not enough, although I made Cord hurry. Bill's .38-40 was just clearing leather when Cord tipped up his holster and shot. Bill's gun thumped when it hit the floor, then he just flowed down after it as though his bones were turning to water.

When I started to get up, Cord said, "Stay there on your hands and knees, Smoke. If you think I won't put a bullet in you, then you think wrong."

He was telling me the truth and I knew it; Cord would kill me as quickly and easily as he would a bad horse. So I stayed there on my hands and knees, not looking at him; I couldn't look at him any more. He moved to the door, then stopped as Julie came out of the hotel across the street. "Bill?" she called. "Where are you, Bill?"

In the silence her voice was clear-toned and strong.

23

I heard Cord leave Lanahan's porch with a rush and jumped to my feet, pumping after him. I banged out, then came to a sudden halt. Cord had crossed the street and was standing near Julie, smiling in his old way.

"Have you seen Bill?" she asked. "I heard a shot as I came down the stairs."

"So did I," Cord said. "That's why I came out, to investigate."

I found my voice at last and yelled, "Run, Julie! Get away from him!"

What I said certainly didn't make sense to her, but the tone was unmistakably urgent. She gave Cord a shocked look, then whirled to run, but he caught her neatly. He had the strength to hold her and he turned so that she was between us.

"Smoke, get back now!"

He started to edge on down the street; I knew he was heading for the stable and his horse. Windows popped open and heads came out and voices demanded to know what the hell was going on. Even Ma looked out and when she saw Cord, she yelled at him, but the words were unintelligible.

The shooting had awakened the town; we were

unaccustomed to firearms going off at four-thirty in the morning. Men appeared wearing only trousers and nightshirts. Julie wasn't struggling; I think she was too frightened to move. Cord was inching his way down the street. He had his hand on his gun and it was pointed at me. When thirty yards separated us, I stepped down from Lanahan's porch, figuring that I was beyond hip-shooting range. My guess was proven correct when Cord fired once but the bullet merely slapped dust five yards to my right.

"Keep back!" he warned. "You don't mean anything to me, Smoke! You're just another man in my way!"

I didn't bother to keep back like he asked; rather, I paced him, taking step for step but keeping my distance. Ponca City was wide-awake and Cord sent them his warning. "Keep clear of me or the girl gets killed!"

They believed him, and I certainly did. He didn't have far to go before he reached the stable, and this worried me, for once he was inside the barn, getting him out would be highly dangerous.

The people of Ponca City were not ones to stand back and let a man shoot up their town. A few ran across to Lanahan's to take a look at Bill Hageman. A moment later a man yelled, "He's alive! Some-one get the doctor! He's alive."

This registered on my mind and I recall feeling vastly relieved, but there wasn't much time for feeling anything else. Men were appearing with rifles and shotguns and Cord had just disappeared into the stable with Julie Hageman.

Around me were the yelling, determined people that I knew so well, and inside the stable was a brother I had only recently gotten to know, an evil man who had no emotion save self-indulgence.

There was no escape for Cord; surely he knew that. In a matter of three minutes the stable was surrounded, while near the front, men began to crowd up behind me. I wanted them there, needed them there, for my fear was almost over-powering. A fear for Julie and my own fear of Cord.

Yet I waved them back and they understood; this was O'Dare business and the O'Dares would handle it their own way. So I stood alone, twenty yards from the black stable maw. Two men with lanterns edged along the wall and hung the lights near the arch. Cord would now have to step into this puddle of brightness in order to escape.

Beneath my coat was Pete Lanahan's .45 Colt; I drew it and cocked it and stood there with its unaccustomed weight in my hand.

From inside the stable, Cord yelled, "Everyone go on home or I'll kill her!"

I was not aware that Ma and Edna had come up behind me to stand on the edge of the crowd.

But Ma yelled, "Smoke, don't hurt him! Please don't hurt him!"

No one else spoke; the town was as silent as Heck Overland's. I could hear Cord stirring around inside the barn. Probably trying to saddle a horse and hold Julie prisoner at the same time.

"Come on out alone, Cord!" I said. "Killing her won't solve anything! It won't save you!"

"Let me walk out and she goes unhurt!"

"You can walk out," I said. "And no one will touch you if you let Julie go. But either way, I'll be standing here. You'll have to walk over me to get away."

He did not answer; I suppose he was thinking it over, but I didn't want him to think; he was too smart for me. "Cord? The place is surrounded, but this is between the O'Dares. I'm your only chance, Cord. And you'll have to kill me to take it."

I wanted to look at Ma, to see if she understood yet about her son, but I didn't dare. She suddenly began to struggle, trying to get to me, but three men held her while Edna did her best to calm her. I stood there for what seemed a long time; actually they tell me it was less than a minute. Then Julie ran out. Two men grabbed her and pulled her to complete safety.

Cord said, "If I throw out my gun, Smoke, do you promise me a trial?"

"The same kind Luther got," I said. "The same

judge. And I'll even hire that lawyer in Guthrie for you."

"Ah," Cord said, "you want to get me hung."

"A chance you got to take," I said. "All I can promise is that I'll be standing here when you step out that door."

"You got a gun, Smoke?"

"I've got a gun."

"You going to shoot me, Smoke?"

That was something I couldn't answer and my silence must have given him some hope. "I've never been mean to you," he said. "And I'm counting on you to remember that, when I step out with empty hands. I don't think you'd shoot an unarmed man." He paused. "Ma! Ma, are you there?"

"I'm here, son!"

"You're not crying, Ma?"

"No," she lied. "I'm not cryin'."

"That's fine. You're my girl, ain't you, Ma?"

"Yes, Cord!"

He laughed, the sound loud in the silence. I swear that I could hear the crowd breathe, so deep was the stillness.

"I was going to give you the world, Ma. Buy you pretty dresses and put a flower in your hair."

"I know, Cord. Cord, you're everything I ever wanted!" She stood there, wringing her hands, tears coursing down her shaking cheeks. "You were always such a good boy. So very good. You minded me so well, like a little angel."

"And you were my first sweetheart," Cord said. "Ma, you know I wouldn't hurt Smoke, don't you, Ma?"

"Yes, yes!"

There was a long silence, too long. "Ma, do you believe the things I did are terrible? Have you really turned against me, Ma?"

"No, no, I'll never believe them. People are always telling lies!"

"Smoke? Smoke, are you still waiting?"

"I'm still here," I said. "The only out is through the door."

"I'm going to throw out my gunbelt," he said. "You watch, Smoke. Don't want you to think I'm trying a trick."

"You throw it and I'll see it," I said.

For a heartbeat I thought he'd changed his mind, then he stepped into the doorway and gave the rig a fling. I watched it plop into the dust and saw the lantern light glance off the nickel-plated .44 Smith & Wesson.

He looked at the crowd, the people he had known for years, but I wondered if he really knew them at all; they certainly didn't know him. He looked at me. Smiled at me. Then he held out his right hand. Twenty yards separated us, or twenty years of lies; anyway it was a gulf I knew I could never bridge.

"Smoke, it's been a time since I've seen you fool with a gun."

"I haven't forgot how to hold it," I said.

"You don't need that with me, boy. You can see that I'm unarmed."

"Then just step over to those fellas so they can put a rope around your wrists." I nodded toward a group standing just at the edge of the lantern light.

"Tie me, Smoke? I wouldn't want to be tied."

"You're going to be," I said. "This is one thing you're not going to get away with, Cord."

"I've always been a man who likes his freedom," he said. "You like freedom too, Smoke."

I did sure enough, but this wasn't the time to talk about it. I'll never know why I suspected him still. Maybe it was that smell of freedom getting into his nose, or maybe he had planned it this way from the first, but when he suddenly ducked his right hand behind him and came up with a small .41 Derringer, I wasn't the least bit surprised.

He had two shots and used them both before I could raise the .45, but he wasted both of them. Could be that the pea-shooter wasn't Cord's kind of gun, or this wasn't his lucky day, because when I dropped the hammer, he spun half around from the bullet's impact. Then I fanned the gun empty as he fell.

I must have hit him three times out of the five but I never knew for sure. I never asked the doctor and he never told me. It made it a little easier, not knowing.

24

The crowd came forward like surf rushing a sandy beach; I just stood there and let them move around me and then I was on the outer fringes and walking toward Pete Lanahan's saloon, his empty .45 in my hand.

Someone was with me, running to keep up, trying to talk to me, but my ears were suddenly plugged and all I could hear was Cord's voice, telling me all the lies that had once meant so much.

Lanahan was alone. He always opened early and was never a man to forsake business on account of a shooting. Experience had taught him that those affairs always worked up an intolerable thirst among the spectators and what better place could be found to toast a winner than in a saloon?

Only there was no toasting; I think I would have killed the man who even suggested one. But Lanahan knew what was good for a man. He passed over a bottle of his best whiskey and I gave him back his gun. While he poured, I studied the grain of the bar, then Lanahan punched out the empties; they sounded like little brass bells when they hit the bare floor.

The whiskey scalded me from throat to toe, and

then I saw that Julie was with me, looking at me, silently offering her help. Only there was little she could do, or anyone for that matter.

A man came in; I think he ran a small shoeshop near the edge of town. He took off his hat and spoke very low to me. "Mr. O'Dare, what shall we do with the—body?"

"Get a wagon from the stable," Julie said. "We'll take him home."

"Yes'm," he said, then started out. At the door he paused and spoke to Julie, as though it were an afterthought. "Your brother's going to be all right, Doc says."

"Thank you," she said, then we were alone again, except for Pete Lanahan, and whoever thinks of a bartender as anything but a fixture. "Smoke," she said, "don't shut me out. Let me help you."

"How can you help?" I wanted to know.

"Let me try, Smoke. Will you let me try?"

I nodded. The foolish dreams I used to carry around in my head suddenly vanished and ahead was a man's world, with a man's trouble, yet I wasn't a bit afraid of it.

"I guess I'd better take Ma and Edna home," I said. "And Cord."

We went out together but parted on the board-walk in front of Lanahan's. Julie was going to stay with her brother at the doctor's house. I walked across the street to the hotel. One of the townsmen had hitched up the buggy and Ma stood under the gallery, wooden-faced, her eyes dead pieces of glass. Edna was with her and when I helped Ma into the rig, she seemed to move in a dream, her expression unchanged.

A man standing near said, "I'll drive the wagon, if that's all right, Smoke."

"Sure," I said, not looking at him. Now I wish I had because I've always wanted to thank him for his kindness but to this day his identity remains a mystery. Edna handed me the reins and I wheeled out of town. Behind us the wagon clattered along and Ma turned on the seat, staring back.

How miserable can a ride be? None more than that, surely. For twenty minutes Ma kept turned around in the seat, looking back. Edna bit her lips until they bled and her fingers plucked her handkerchief to ribbons.

"Luther'll be home soon," I said, hoping this would swing Ma's mind away from the wagon and Cord stretched out in back.

"He won't stay," Edna said dully. "Not when he finds out about me."

"What about you?" I asked. "As I remember you telling me, it was love at first sight."

She began to cry with alarming suddenness, but her voice was full of hope, and thanks. "Smoke, do you mean that? Do I get this chance?"

"What the devil are you talking about?" I said and settled back to the driving.

Ma surprised me when she turned around properly on the seat and said, "He was oldest, my first-born. I remember how I held him, how I just knew that he'd be a great man someday. But he was going to kill my youngest. Stand there, laughing and killing."

I wondered if I should say anything, to try to tell her how I felt, but then I decided that she knew and understood and that I was never going to have to talk about it. During those last moments in Cord's life he had lied to her, used her love for him; she knew this now and it must have been a terrible burden on her heart.

So I remained silent, understanding then that a woman's grief is often unspeakable, yet men offend it with hollow words.

She said no more and at the home place I got down and went around to help her. She puffed on to the house, placing her hand on each thigh to help hoist her bulk up the porch steps. The man who had driven the wagon parked it by the barn. He came up and said something to Edna about covering Cord good, then left, riding one of the horses he had unhitched.

Ma was moving around the house, putting a match to the lamps. Edna started to go in, but I said, "Wait. Not yet."

"I don't think it's safe to leave her alone," Edna said.

"We're all alone, all of us," I said. "Even when

we think we're in a crowd, we're still alone. Ma'll find her way out."

And I think she did. She came out of the house with a bundle of old newspapers and placed them in the yard, near the porch. Then she carried out some kindling and arranged it neatly. Edna and I watched, but I don't think Ma even knew we were there.

She made another trip, only this time she had changed into an old housedress, carrying in her arms the velvet gift from Cord. One by one she brought out all those things he had given her, piled them together over the kindling, then put a match to the whole thing and watched them burn. Curling skyward was a banner of smoke, fed by the hollow gifts he had given so he could silently laugh. But the fire burned quickly, soon reducing itself to a small mound of hot ash, the last remaining vestige of Cord's magnificent hate for all mankind.

I envied her; my memories wouldn't be burned to ashes and scatter to the wind.

Finally Ma stepped onto the porch. She looked at Edna and me and said, "You ought to come in before you catch cold. We'll have to bury Cord in the morning."

Edna went with her; it is a woman's place to comfort women. I sat on the steps and waited for the dawn wind to die. It would; I could bet on it for I lived in an unchanging world. Tomorrow, after the service, I'd go in to meet Bud Ledbetter and bring Luther home.

Maybe Julie too, if the preacher was available.

Anyway, it was something to think about.

Center Point Large Print
600 Brooks Road / PO Box 1
Thorndike, ME 04986-0001 USA

(207) 568-3717

US & Canada:
1 800 929-9108
www.centerpointlargeprint.com

Los Alamos County Library
2400 Central Avenue
Los Alamos, NM 87544

WITHDRAWN